SLICES OF LIFE

ALSO BY
Emmitte Hall

BOOKS:

Dead Ends-Twisted Tales and Nasty Endings Volume I
Grave Digger Blues-Twisted Tales and Nasty Endings Volume II
Articles-Past Published Non-Fics

AMAZON.COM/SHORTS
The Obliquity of the Ecliptic

ONE ACT PLAYS
The Keys to Nevermore
The Game
The Fear

TEN MINUTE PLAYS
Scratch-Off Sally
The Ex-Pats
The Comet
Speeding
The Invisible Elephant
Stood Up

REALLY SHORT PLAYS
A Royal Pain
Acquaintances
Stranded
The Pitcher
The Carney
Satan Dreams
Little Angels
Gangsta

www.emmittehall.com

SLICES OF LIFE

Twisted Tales and Nasty Endings Volume III

by

Emmitte Hall

iUniverse, Inc.
New York   Bloomington

Slices of Life
Twisted Tales and Nasty Endings Volume III

iUniverse books may be ordered through booksellers or by contacting:

iUniverse
1663 Liberty Drive
Bloomington, IN 47403
www.iuniverse.com
1-800-Authors (1-800-288-4677)

ISBN: 978-1-4401-4771-5 (pbk)
ISBN: 978-1-4401-4772-2 (ebook)

Printed in the United States of America

iUniverse rev. date: 8/03/09

For Norma, Jerry, Ed and Dave

GUY
I'm just a glorified extra, Fred. I'm a dead man anyway. If I'm going to die, I'd rather go out a hero than a coward.

FRED
Maybe you're the plucky comic relief, you ever think of that?

Galaxy Quest
by
David Howard
Robert Gordon

God doesn't play dice.

-Albert Einstein

Contents

▼

I

▼

SCRAPBOOKING
FOR CANNIBALS

Tuesday night scrapbook party at Mildred's, 2211 Hide Away lane, 7:30 pm. sharp. Friends together with wine and cheese and tasty little snacks and the opportunity to trade memories of old friends and new acquaintances. Beatrice would be there tonight with boxes of new scrapbooking tools, pattern scissors, crinkle cutters, alphabet forms, heavy-duty cutting knives, acid free papers and thick new books to paste all the memories in.

Everyone looked forward to Mildred's Tuesday Night's Scrapbooking parties. The women chatted and gossiped about the juicy details of their latest adventures. Mildred wore her beige leather pantsuit that she had sewn herself. Janie wore black as always with bleached, bone colored buttons. Felicia liked to wear imports, something from Europe or Spain. She especially liked things from France, not because of quality or design but because it made a political statement. Mildred hated things from France and complained that she could never get "the smell" out.

Anticipation filled the air tonight as Shannon was bringing a new girl. The two finally arrived at 7:45 and she introduced her friend as Mona, a very nice, plump woman of about 45. She looked to weigh over 400 pounds and had rolls upon rolls of soft, smooth flesh overflowing her bright flowered dress, and she had beautiful blue eyes.

Janie led her to the couch and everyone surrounded the new guest and welcomed her to the group. Mildred poured her a tall glass of sweet red wine and they all peppered her with questions:

"Where do you live?" "Where do you work?" "Are you married?" "Do you have family here?" "How many kids do you have?" "Where do you get your hair done?" "I love that dress" and other things like that.

"I just moved here from Chicatilo, grew up there," Mona said turning and nodding at all her new friends.

"Really and where is that?" asked Felicia lighting up a long cigarette and stretching out along the top of the sofa very close to Mona. .

"It's a small town south of Shawcross, over in Hinsdale County. I really liked it there, but I just couldn't stay there after my divorce, too many bad memories."

"Ohhh, so sorry to hear about that, my dear," Felecia said, blowing a big cloud of smoke into the air.

"It's alright," she said coughing, "things are going to be better now, I can feel it. My husband used to beat me," she confessed and tears welled up in her eyes on this confession.

"Oh, that's awful, he didn't leave marks, did he?" asked Janie.

"No, no marks or bruises," she answered to everyone's relief, "he was very abusive, physically, verbally, emotionally and sometimes even sexually."

"Really," everyone said at once. Felecia leaned forward and said, "tell us more."

"You know, after living with someone for 4 years, you'd think you'd know them, see something like this coming," she said and dabbed the corners of her eyes with a napkin. Her thick mascara smeared leaving clown tracks on her face.

"Do you really ever know somebody?" Janie said.

Mona sobbed and said, "I'm sorry, I really didn't mean to get into all of this…"

"No, its fine" said Mildred, gently patting her on the shoulder.

"Yes, its fine, you've been through a lot" said Janie.

"I guess the wounds of separation and divorce are still raw right now…"

"Wounds!" Felicia said.

"The wounds of divorce," Janie said through clinched teeth.

"Oh, sorry, do go on," Felicia said blowing smoke.

"Really, it's all right, thank you so much for listening, you have all been so very kind," Mona said.

"Well, you are among friends tonight," said Mildred and everyone agreed.

"Thank you" Mona said and looked at her pudgy hands in her lap. She looked so sad and dejected and everyone tried not to laugh at her fat clown face.

"Have something to eat, that will make you feel better and Beatrice should be here any moment and we can start scrapbooking," said Mildred and handed her a plate with assorted crackers and toppings. Mona took several and put them on her napkin briefly before stuffing them into her face and washing them down with wine.

"Where did you and Shannon meet?" asked Mildred.

"Shannon is the greatest," Mona smiled. "She was with the town's Welcome Wagon. I just moved into my apartment and she came by with a bag of coupons and brochures and pens and those rubber jar openers from the community merchants and well, we just got to talking like we were lost sisters. It was uncanny."

"It's almost too good to be true," Felecia said, smiling widely.

"When Shannon found out I was alone here, no family or friends, she invited me to your party," Mona said, looking at her new friends.

"Good ole Shannon, a truer friend is rare indeed," said Janie.

"Yes, very rare," Felicia said with a smile.

"To Shannon" said Janie and held her wine glass in the air. The ladies of the Tuesday Night Scrapbooking Club lifted their glasses high and clinked them all together. Mona seemed near tears again and Felicia sipped her wine into her cheeks and held it until the urge to laugh had passed.

"Oh, these are very good, what is it?" said Mona, stuffing more crackers into her mouth

"There's some pate and various cheeses and some Libdomen," said Felicia and everyone quickly gave her dirty looks which she ignored.

"It's all delicious," she said and stuffed some more in her mouth. "What is Libdomen?"

"Ah, Libdomen is a deadly predator my husband hunts up north each winter…" said Mildred, glaring at Felicia.

"It's very good, can I have some more?"

Mildred passed the tray to her and Janie filled Mona's glass with more wine.

"Felicia, where did you get that dress, it's very unusual" asked Mona through a mouthful of crackers and cheese.

"Do you like it?" she asked.

"Yes, yes I do."

"Its leather, I made it myself. Touch it," she invited.

Felicia walked over and stood close to Mona and let her run her hands over the smooth, cool texture of the dress.

"I've never felt anything like it," said Mona, "where did you get it?"

"It's French, darling," she said and pressed Mona's face gently into her breasts.

"Ah, let me have the tray and I'll go and get us some more snacks," said Mildred, "and Janie, would you get Mona some more wine?"

Felicia walked away and lit another cigarette.

"No, I'm getting a little light headed already, I don't think I need any more wine," Mona said with a big grin.

"Non-sense," said Janie, "Shannon here will take good care of you, tonight is girl's night out." Mona handed Janie her glass and she filled it with more dark red wine.

Mildred went through the swinging doors into the kitchen. Her husband Leonard sat at the kitchen table drinking a can of beer and reading the paper. He was a big man in denim bib overalls and a white t-shirt.

"We need some more Libdomen," she said and spread assorted crackers across the silver serving tray. "That woman eats a lot."

"Yeah, she's a big girl, a really big girl," he said and picked up a large carving knife from the counter top.

"Felicia is really pushing it tonight too, you should hear some of the things she's saying."

"Well, she always pushes the limits." He opened the large walk-in freezer at the back of the kitchen. Harry Libdomen, Leonard's ex-boss hung from a meat hook at the back of the freezer. Leonard cut thin slices from Libdomen's right shoulder and set the thin slivers into a bowl. Harry was half the man he used to be as most of the meat from his legs and left side were gone. Libdomen had been a hulking, violent man who liked to verbally intimidate and abuse his employees. The last time he yelled at Leonard, he woke up in Mildred's meat locker, hanging from a hook. He screamed for days, then begged to die, then died quietly in the freezer. Leonard was tired of looking at his ex-bosses bloated face and opaque eyes, besides, the meat was going stale.

"Libdomen's getting freezer burn. It's time to toss him," he said and dropped the finely carved flesh into the cast iron skillet Mildred had on the stove.

"It looks like we might have some fresh meat tonight, Lenny," Mildred said, turning the thin slivers of flesh in the hot skillet.

Leonard went back to reading the paper and Mildred heated up Mr. Libdomen and cut him up for crackers and sprinkled on some cheese and spices and carried the plate to the guests.

"Fresh snacks," she said just as the door bell rang.

Everyone paused at once and looked at one another and then at the door.

"You Hoo, it's me Beatrice, open the door," the perky voice from the other side of the door said and everyone grinned. Janie downed her wine and poured herself another and filled Mona's glass at the same time.

Mildred peeked through the door's spy hole. Beatrice stood on the front porch in a blue pant suit. Mildred opened the door for Beatrice who rushed in like a perfumed storm, pulling a dolly full of boxes and cases. "Hello everyone! How is everybody?" She pushed the dolly up against the wall and gave Mildred a big hug. She wore a half a dozen slender silver bracelets that tinkled like wind chimes with every move.

"Shannon, glad to see you, and Felicia, you look great as usual, love that dress!"

"Thank you" said Felicia.

"Janie" Beatrice said with a glance, "and who is this precious creature?" she asked and approached Mona who struggled against the wine and the weight to stand.

"I'm Mona, Shannon's friend," she said.

"Very glad to meet you Mona," Beatrice said and took Mona's hand in both of hers and shook them vigorously. Beatrice held her hand in hers and looked Mona over with a wide smile.

"It's good to meet you too," Mona said, swaying slightly. Janie handed her a glass of wine.

"Well now," she said and finally releasing Mona's hand. "Is everyone ready to scrapbook?"

"Yes, we can't wait," said Shannon.

"I have some wonderful new things to show you tonight," Beatrice said and pulled a box off the top of the dolly and pulled out a cutter with a round blade resembling a pizza cutter.

"Please pass the wine around and everyone top off your glass before we get started," Mildred, the consummate hostess said.

"This is new in a line of edgers that comes in a variety of patterns, the pattern shape is etched in the top of the handle," Beatrice explained and turned the knife handle around so everyone could see. "This makes cutting large pieces easy, fun and attractive. Next we have a tattoo box," she pulled a 5x7 inch shadow box out and showed everyone.

"This comes in a variety of standard sizes from 3x5 to 11x16 and you can special order other sizes also ladies, you will love this, the Back Splash is a large thoracic sized frame to mount those total back tattoos."

Mona sat sipping wine and listened with a confused look on her face.

"Next we have some carving knives from the Ed Gein Collection, it comes in the home and professional editions. They are a little pricey, but you really can't beat the quality. Next we have a new line of canopic jars." She pulled a notebook out and held up 8x10 colored photos of each design as she explained, "we have the traditional Egyptian jars, very chic and the new cookie jar collection, shaped like cats and pigs and cartoon characters. I think you'll love these wildly colored retro designs from Karl Denke. See? Next, I have some killer close out prices on the Hospital Collection, these are your standard clear jars with sealed metal lids. These are great from Med-students and science minded scrap bookers, of course, it just requires a little discretion. Simple, functional. Each jar comes with a receipt addressed from Torrid's Gag Shop in San Francisco to help you answer any unwanted questions."

Mona looked a little pale and seemed to sway a little on the couch. "What… what are, is, all this stuff for?" she asked, her words heavy from the wine.

"Ah, Beatrice, our new guest is not up to speed on our particular hobby, she was invited more as a craft project than as a new member," said Felicia.

"Oh, I see" said Beatrice.

"What do you mean, craft project?" asked Mona through a hiccup.

"Here, let me hold your wine for you, Mona, you don't look so good," Shannon said and took her wine glass from her.

"Thanks, I don't feel very good, I think I'm getting a headache."

Leonard came out of kitchen carrying a large rubber mallet and whacked her on the head. Mona fell unconscious to the floor.

Beatrice shrugged, "I'm sorry, I didn't know she was dinner, I thought she was a new member."

Janie glared at Beatrice and said, "what were you thinking, even if she was invited as a guest, look at that skin, rolls and rolls of it, we would have turned her into a canvas before dessert, even if she was likable."

"I brought her, I get first choice" Shannon insisted.

Leonard wrapped Mona's head in plastic to control the bleeding and stop the breathing. He struggled to drag her into the kitchen. "Hey, Beatrice, can I borrow your dolly?"

"Sure, go ahead."

Leonard pushed the body onto the dolly and hauled her into the kitchen.

"Ok, ladies, let's scrapbook."

Felicia placed a shoe box on the coffee table and opened it up. Everyone peeked inside and let out a little laugh. "I get this stuff from my brother-in-law over in the Middle East, bits and pieces from suicide bombers and little terrorists, help yourself," she said and they all reached in as if it were a box of chocolates. "I can get a ton of this stuff, thought about advertising on E-Bay but don't know how 'Severed Ear for sale' would look on the internet."

"I bet it would sell," said Janie. "You could make a fortune."

"I can place orders too, if you want something special just let me know and allow 2-4 weeks for delivery."

"Beatrice," shouted Leonard from the kitchen, "where's that big pot, I can't find it."

"Did you clean it up last time?" Beatrice shouted back.

"No."

"Well then, look in the garage. You might have to use the Safari crock, she's a pretty big girl, it's out in the shed next to the axe grinder."

"Thank Hon," he called back and they heard the door slam.

"I don't think she'll be ready tonight girls, we might have to do this next week," said Mildred.

"My grandson is coming over next week for his birthday, he likes coming to Grandma's for his cake and ice cream," said Beatrice.

"Ok, how about the week after that?" asked Mildred.

"That's fine with me," said Felicia.

"Me too," said Janie.

"Yeah, whatever," said Shannon. "I've got to go, I'll see you in two weeks." She picked up her case and put a couple of terrorist parts into a plastic bag and left.

"What's her problem?" asked Beatrice.

"She seems bored," said Janie.

"I don't think she's having fun anymore" said Mildred.

"Shannon likes the hunt more than the time we spend scrapbooking," said Felicia. "She mentioned to me she wants to leave the group, join Deidra's Collector's Club."

"Don't they meet on Thursday nights?" asked Mildred.

"Those serial killers are a bunch of bitches," Janie said.

"Leave the group and give up scrapbooking?" said Beatrice.

"Yeah, she and her new friends will hunt one, sometimes two people a night," Janie said.

"Do they?" asked Mildred.

"Yeah, haven't you been watching the news, they've gotten six this month and a four month old is missing, someone picked up a baby right out of a shopping cart at Kirk's on Devine street," said Janie.

"Devine street, isn't that over where you live?" asked Felicia.

"Yes, it is," said Beatrice, "that's too close to home."

"Well, that's not good. I think maybe she needs to be voted out" said Felicia.

"Shannon's been scrapbooking with us since we started the club, she started the Welcome Wagon to recruit new projects." said Beatrice.

"But she's getting reckless and that endangers all of us," Mildred said, "all those in favor of terminating Janie's membership say yeah." Everyone said yeah, "all those opposed," silence. "Ok, next meeting she's gone. I'll tell Leonard, I'm going to miss her.

"Me too," said Janie.

"Ok, well, who's got something to share with out today?" asked Beatrice.

"I made a scrapbook from that hotel fire over off Custer lane last month," said Felicia.

"That fire at the hotel? Wasn't that where all the doors were blocked off?" asked Mildred.

"Yes, the sprinkler system was shut off and the fire doors were barricaded shut' said Felicia, grinning."

"Do you know anything about that, Madame Felicia" asked Mildred.

"I plead the fifth," she said and she opened the memories book and turned the pages to show off pictures of burning victims and other souvenirs.

II

▼

THE FACTORY

A Graphic Novel Trapped in .txt

Distant View-An expansive Factory looms large above a crowded city. The colors are dark and dull and dirty.
Hundreds of smokestacks of varying sizes and heights are packed tightly behind the tall stone walls of the Factory. The smoke stacks belch thick black smoke into an already thick gray sky. Two-story square buildings sit among the smokestacks, their large black windows look like unseeing eyes. Narrow concrete roads snake throughout the factory for cars and trucks. No people are seen, there is no apparent activity, just the billowing of smoke from the tall smoke stacks.

Closer View-Factory
A lone man is seen walking down an empty road inside the Factory, barely visible among the buildings and tall cylinders. He is tall and hunched and dirty. He looks small surrounded by the gray towers of the Factory.

Closer View-Man
He is old, looks older than his years. He wears a faded blue coverall, dull with dirt and sweat and time. He wears a dirty yellow hard hat and heavy dark work boots. In his right hand he is carrying a metal lunch pail, curved on top like a barn. He is a big, muscular man, with powerful hands.

Close Up-Name Badge
On his chest, a dingy oval name badge sewn above the left pocket of his overalls says "219-6874328."

Time Clock-Time Card Rack
219 stands at a wall with hundreds of metal pockets for time cards. There is only one. He pulls his time card out and inserts it into a slot on the punch clock. It is seven o'clock. He puts his time card back where he got it.

Time Clock-Door
There is a door next to the time clock, but it is closed. In a wooden pocket on the door is a single sheet of paper. 219 retrieves it.

Close Up-Work Order
The paper in 219's hand is smudged and dirty and crinkled. In thick black grease pencil is a row of numbers and letters:

A-52	R2-9283
J-6423	BC-3254
L-9124-9175	RT3-4329
GF-44944a	E-918-996
R-5432	F-1234
XT-956235	P-8945
RJ-6000	Z-3256
JR-1006	KL-3254
B2F-999	UTI-3254

Distant Shot-219 walking into the Factory
219 shuffles down the winding concrete road towards one of the two story buildings. Building B-9.

Wide Shot-Inside building
The building is one large room with rows of lunchroom style tables and stools that connect to the table. The room is dark, a small amount of light seeps through the dirty windows. There is trash, old coffee cups, dirty plates and manuals scattered across the tops of the tables and on the floor. Trash cans in the corners overflow with refuse. Along the walls are rows of lockers, stacked two high.

Close Up-Lockers
219 walks across the room, to the center row and opens up locker 219.

Close Up-Locker 219
Inside is a large crescent wrench, three foot long and heavy. It is caked with dirt. 219 pulls it out and puts his lunch pail in.

Wide Shot-B-9 in the back ground
219 is walking away from building B-9 in the distance, we get a rare glimpse of the lines and soot and the despair on 219's face.

Work Order
219 holds the work order in his hand and in the distance we see towering skeletal structures made of gray I-Beams. The steel support beams shoot up and across and at angles as far as the eye can see.

Wide Shot-Steel Beam A
Steel Beam A is two stories above the ground and marked with a large A. In each I-Beam are a number of large hexagonal nuts, each with a number above it.

Close Up-A-52
The wrench is on nut A-52. The large hand of 219 clenches the wrench.

Close Up-Face of 219
219 strains and sweats as he attempts to tighten nut A-52.

Wide Shot of Steel Structure
Wide shot of the I-Beam structure as 219 climbs down.

Wide Shot-219 and Steel Structure
219 is a walking towards the reader, tired and bent, the tall, straight structure looms behind him.

Two Page Montage
Close ups of R-5432, RJ-6000, UTI-3254, KL-3254, the wrench, the hand, the straining face as he works to tighten each nut and works his way through the Factory.

Distant Shot-219 walking towards the Time Clock
219 walks through the gray Factory towards the time clock.

Close Up-Hand
219 reaches for his time card

Close Up-Hand
Hand puts time card back into time card pocket

Wide Shot-Factory and town
219 walks out of the factory towards home as the sun sets through the smog.

Close Up-Time Clock
The time clock says it is ten minutes before seven.

Wide Shot-Town and factory, the sun is rising
In the distance, against the town in the background and the Factory in the foreground, a lone figure walks towards the factory.

Time Clock-Time Card Rack
219 stands at a wall with metal pockets for time cards. He pulls his time card and punches it. It is seven o'clock.

Time Clock-Door
There is a door next to the time clock. He picks the piece of paper from a wooden pocket on the door.

Close Up-Work Order
The paper in 219's hand is smudged and dirty and crinkled. In thick black grease pencil is a row of numbers and letters:

A-52	R-921
ST-6423	BCI-3254
KJ-9124	RTDC-4329
F-44	EXP-918
RRE-5432	F19-1234
TX-9562	P2P-945

RIG-602   LMN-256

RJ-1006   KIL-5431

F3B-999   XXX-2666

Distant Shot-219 walking into the Factory
219 shuffles into Building B-9.

Wide Shot-Inside building B-9

Close Up-Lockers

Close Up-Locker 219
219 pulls his large crescent wrench from the locker.

Wide Shot-B-9 in the back ground
219 is walking away from building B-9 in the distance.

Work Order
219 holds the work order in his hand A beam is in the distance, nut 52 is clearly seen.

Close Up-A-52
The wrench is on nut A-52. The large hand of 219 clenches the wrench.

Close Up-Face of 219
219 strains and sweats as he attempts to tighten nut A-52.

Wide Shot of Steel Structure
Wide shot of the I-Beam structure as 219 climbs down.

Wide Shot-219 and Steel Structure
219 is a walking towards the reader, tired and bent, the tall, straight structure looms behind him.

Close Up Shots-Face, hand and wrench
219 is working straining to tighten the nuts in several close up shots.

Wide Shot of Beam XXX-2666
219 looks up at the towering structure against the gray sky

Medium Shot-219 climbing structure
The structure is tall, Beam XXX is near the top.

Close Up-Face
219 is straining and sweating to get to the top

Close up-Nut XXX-2666
Close up of Nut, the town and the factory in the distance

Close Up-Wrench on Nut
219 is straining to tighten the nut, the muscles in his dirty arm are tight and strained.

Close Up-Wrench and Hand
The hand has slipped and there is a large gash 219's hand and he is bleeding profusely.

Medium Shot of 219 high up on structure
219 pulls a dirty handkerchief from his pocket and wraps it around his hand

Medium Shot of 219 on the Structure
He climbs down the structure

Medium Shot-Time Clock
He punches the time clock with his wrapped up hand, blood soaking through.

Wide Shot-219 leaving the Factory
He leaves the Factory, lunch pail in hand, hand bandaged and dark with blood, walking home, the Factory large behind him, the town, gray and sooty before him.

Medium Shots-Town
219 walks down treeless streets lined with identical box homes in varying degrees of disrepair. There are no people.

Medium Shot-House
He walks up the littered path towards his home, the windows are dark.

Wide Shot-Interior of Home
The house is sparsely furnished, a ragged couch, a torn up recliner in front of a TV with an antennae on top. The floor is littered with cups and discarded bags of fast food. There are darkened doors off this room, but we cannot tell what they are.

Wide Shot of Bathroom
The bathroom is dingy, gray, 219 pulls the bandage from his hand and it squirts blood.

Medium Shot-Arm over sink
He washes the gaping wound in the sink

Close Up of Arm
Gaping Wound

Medium Shot-Bathroom
He wraps in his hand in a towel

Medium Shot-Living room
He flops on the couch, the room is only lit by the glow of the TV.

Close up of Face
He is in pain, sweating.

Close Up of Face
He is sleeping.

Montage
219 is sleeping, rolling around on the couch as the clock in the background, and the changing of the light from day to night, shows that several days have passed.

Close Up-Clock
It is 6am.

Close Up-Face
219 is asleep

Close Up-Face
219 is awake

Medium Shot-219 walking down street towards Factory
219 is walking slowly to work, his lunch pail in his hand, the Factory looms large in front of him.

Distant Shot-219 walking towards the Time Clock
219 walks through the gray Factory towards the time clock.

Close Up-Hand
219 reaches for his time card

Close Up-Time Clock
A bandaged hand punches the time clock, it is seven o'clock.

Close Up-Hand
Hand puts time card back into time card pocket

Close Up-Door beside time card
The door is shut as usual. The slot is filled with work orders.

Close Up of Hand
Reaching for work orders.

Close Up-Work order
Top of work order is A-52

Close Up-Hand
Hand reaching into locker to get large wrench out, the lunch pail is in the locker, his arm is bandaged.

Medium Shot-219 in front of A-Structure
219 looks up towards the massive A-Structure, wrench in one hand, work orders in the other.

Close up of Work Order
A-52

Closer Shot of Work Order
A-52

Large Close Up of Work Order
A-52

Close up of Nut A-52
219 beats the nut with his wrench

Close ups and wide shots of 219
Beating nut A-52 with his wrench, sweat pours from his face and he keeps hitting it.

Close up of wrench on A-52
219 strains to loosen the nut

Close up of 219's face
He strains to loosen nut

Close up of A-52
Nut loosens

Wide shot of 219 on top of A-Structure
219 pulls the nut from the bolt and beats the bolt with his wrench

Close up of bolt
Bolt pounds out

Medium Shot Bolt
Bolt falling through the air against the backdrop of the Factory

Medium Shot of 219 on top of A-Structure
219 flings the nut into the far distance of the Factory

Medium Shot
A-Structure starts to shake

Close up of Face
219 is scared as the structure begins to shake

Wide Shot of 219
Scurrying down A-Structure as it shakes violently

Medium Shot of 219 Running Away
A-Structure is behind him and shaking as he runs away

Wide Shot 219 Running
The Factory is behind him and A-Structure falters and falls

Wide Shot of Factory
The whole Factory is shaking and falling apart

Wide Shot of Factory-219 running
The whole factory falls apart and is in a big pile of ruins, smoke billowing from the center.

Medium Shot of 219 at Time Clock
219 punches out

Medium Shot 219-Factory behind him
219 is slinking off, concern on his greasy face, the factory behind him in ruins.

III

▼

THE SPIDER

Thank you Mr. Johnson, Mr. Jeffers and Mr. Jeffreys for seeing me today. My name is Paul Paulson, and on behalf of Peppenopolis' Perfect Prunes, I want to thank you for the opportunity to present our prunes to you for consideration for inclusion in J & J Supermarket chain. Peppenopolis' Perfect Prunes are produced right here in Pennsylvania, we plant our prunes in the perfect soil and pick them only when they are plump and ripe. Soon after these sweet things are sun dried and sent fresh to your produce section.

"Paul, what are you doing up so late?" Patricia, Paul's wife stood at the doorway plenty pissed.

"I've got a big presentation in the morning to J&J Supermarket chain and I'm just working on my presentation."

"It's 2 a.m."

"It's a big account. If I can get our prunes into J & J, it could mean a lot of commission money for me, for us."

"You won't be able to sell sun tan lotion on the sun if you don't get some sleep."

"I'll be there in a few minutes, I'm too nervous to sleep; you know how I get before a big presentation."

Patricia turned and went to bed.

Paul continued on his presentation.
My prunes are pit-less...Peppenopolis Prunes are pit-less, pit-less prunes...Peppenopolis' prunes are pure, plump and pit-less, are pitted, de-pitted...don't have pits...

Peppenopolis Perfect Pickled Peppers

Paul paused, he heard something, a distant clicking, perhaps a tapping, as if there was something gently rapping somewhere near the floor. He looked towards the door, but Pat was there no more. He listened even closer still, he heard the humming of the heater, the flow of air across the grate, the swinging of the pendulum in the grandfather clock, the creaking of the house as it settled.

People prefer pit-less prunes, it prevents people for choking and they can enjoy the whole prune. People who eat prunes with pits waste 10-40% of the prune, depriving them of the valuable nutrients and minerals such as A, B, C and D vitamins that are plentiful in prunes.

Something in the corner caught his eye, a movement, perhaps a shadow passing, something from the corner of his eye, just beyond his peripheral vision and then the clicking/tapping started too but there was nothing there.

Prunes are the perfect fruit, packed with goodness

The clicking started once again. He scanned the room, he looked towards the doors, he searched the crevices on the floor, and there he spied a spider scurrying in the corner. It seemed to leap, as if trying to reach some unseen goal, a place above the floor, a crevice in which to scale the wall, and as he tried to climb and fall and rush to find another place to climb, with each step Paul heard the click of its tiny legs upon the tile. The spider paused as if detected, as if it knew it had been seen.

The spider ceased its attempt to climb and turned around and stared at Paul. Its long legs arched as if to pounce, and if in attitude it thought it could leap the seven feet and land on top of Paul. It swayed from side to side on quad sets of hairy legs and then leaned forward as if in challenge. Paul stared with some concern and then returned to his speech about the prunes, glancing occasionally at the brown arachnid. The spider turned and resumed its quest to scale the pebbled wall. Paul glanced around the upper corners of the room in search of the silken strands of a spider web, a home, a meal, the spider's quest, a sack of eggs that held a thousand tiny legs, ready to burst into the den at any moment. With each step the clicking sounded, as Paul watched, astounded.

How could he hear such things, the click of tiny feet, (if a spider has indeed such things) or simply tips of legs upon the cold, tile floor, or the subtle bump of its thorax on the ground? The spider stopped and turned again and charged two feet towards him and stopped.

Paul, embarrassed turned back to speech about plump prunes and in a moment heard the spider's steps recede and the clicking, bumping sound returned as the hairy creature tried again to find a hold and scurry up the wall.

He watched but dared not stare as the spider seemed to sense his spying eyes, but yet the sales pitch about the prunes no longer flowed, grew flat, the volume of the spider's footsteps grew with every ounce of added concentration. And yet the spider too pursued his quest as Paul continued his, honing his perfect pitch and forgot the spider soon.

And that is why, ladies and gentleman, Pepperpolopis's Perfect Prunes are perfect for your store.

Paul finished and felt his perfect speech would surely sell a bunch of prunes, but quickly found a typo in a paragraph began his search for more. His eyes grew tired and his brain got bored and he searched the wall to find the spider. He looked, he searched, his listened quite intently and was soon rewarded with the sound of something quickly scurrying, and there it was, the tiny spider running right along the baseboards behind the television set. Paul watched and waited and soon the tiny spider ran towards the other corner, stopping there again it searched and waited as if expected some sign or special invitation and assistance in its quest to climb the wall. It jumped and rushed and ran, bumping walls and floors and corners.

The noise it made, while quiet as the wind, blew through his nerves like claws across a chalk board.

"Enough," Paul said and found the front page neatly folded beside him on the couch. He picked it up and scanned the headlines and finding nothing rolled the paper even tighter and walked slowly towards the spider as if tracking wild cats in the woods.

The spider now he saw was rather small, brown and black with tiny hairy legs and nothing indicating venom. He leaned closer, ever closer and more slowly, and careful not to cast a shadow to alert his hairy prey. The spider seemed to sense him and stopped and turned in time to be struck by page one, section one, firmly and decisively. Paul stepped back and saw the spider curled into a ball, its legs bent oddly and the body still.

"Ding Dong, the spiders gone," he chimed and sat back at his tablet, editing.

He'd always wanted to sell strawberries, fresh grapes and plums and leave the world of processed and pitted prunes behind. He never liked the way they smelled and never ate them in his pitches. The smooth glass jars that held the wrinkled fruit seemed so cold, so impersonal, like little shrunken heads floating in a jar in some touristy souvenir store. But tomorrow he would present his most important sales event and could not dream of better days ahead. One day though he would go into a client and pull his paring knife and cut thick wedges of fresh melons, red strawberries and plums and pass the fragrant fruit around the room and simply smile, for who could pass on that. But prunes he quickly found were best left in jars or better yet, pictures of the prunes, enlarged and wet, for the promise of the fruit was far better.

He set his pencil down and rubbed his eyes a bit and looking up, he found the spider gone. He looked around the crevices and along the baseboards, and saw nothing. He had not heard his hairy friend depart and thought him dead, as he had been beaten by the headline news.

The hour was late and his eyes grew heavy and he needed to put his head upon the pillow in order to get a few hours rest and he gently laid his head against the couch and dreamed of peach trees on a hot summer day. And then he felt the gentle touch as if a lover's breathe upon his ear and turning towards the naked sound he saw the big brown spider. It leaped onto his head and hid beneath the tussle of his hair. Paul jumped up and shook his head and ran his fingers through the strands and propelled the spider to the floor and he watched it scurry beneath a chair before he could squash it with his stockinged foot.

Paul's heart beat fast and he perspired and he sat to rest a moment. It had no right to intrude into his house and invade his night. He had important work to do and hunting spiders was not among the lists. He sat and listened and turned his attention once again to his notes and waited. The spider did not appear and he soon tired of the game, he had to think about the prunes and stared intently at his paper.

A moment, a minute, perhaps just seconds passed and then it appeared along the top, the spider on the speech. It stared at him and Paul starred back before he flung it across the room. In a panic he let the papers fly and with it, the creature too. The papers floated to the ground like dried leaves in winter and Paul stomped on each of the papers, trying to grind the spider into the floor, he had not seen where the spider went to.

Each paper he lifted slowly, expecting spider goo beneath each one and finding none he lifted the others until he came to the last one and as soon as he pulled the paper from the floor, the spider charged him, scurrying rapidly towards Paul's feet, and Paul jumped back and tripped and teetered backwards onto his back, his legs and arms flailing in the air like a cockroach near death. He put his feet back on the ground and tried to catch his breath and then he felt the fingers cold like ice as the spider crawled up past his sock and up his leg. Paul jumped and stomped and could not dislodge the bug. He slapped and patted his pant leg all around and still the spider climbed and Paul was near a panic as he waited for the spider's fangs to dig into his flesh. He undid his belt and popped the button, pulled the zipper down and shed his pants as quickly as he could. The spider stood beneath his groin and seemed to grin grin he bit him in the leg.

Paul screamed in pain and Pat ran in and saw her husband nearly naked in the den, a small brown stain below his briefs, she stared at him and shook her head, then turned and returned to bed. Paul saw his papers scattered, smudged and ripped and tattered on the floor and were of no use to him anymore. His leg began to ache and swell and the ice he applied as painful and uncomfortable as any bite he'd had. He collected the tattered pieces of his speech and saw the words were unreadable and tossed the useless papers in the trash.

He sat back on the couch and let his head rest upon the pillows. He heard the ticking of the clock and knew the night was nearly gone, he listened to the drip of water coming from the leaky kitchen sink and then spied the silken spider web laced across one corner of the room, a small egg sack hanging there. It quivered, it shook and seemed to grow then burst loudly like a balloon and the tiny bodies of a thousand spiders rained down across the room and then he heard the tiny feet, could feel the rumble of the floor, of a thousand tiny spiders coming forth.

Paul died right there, as much from spider bites as fright and despair, his pitch on prunes discarded and scattered and the tiny spiders feasted, ready to go out into the world to spin their own webs and dreams.

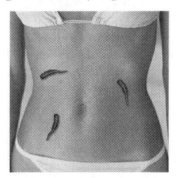

IV

▼

END OF THE LINE

Gerald Stern arrived at 1414 Washington Avenue 30 minutes early. He paid the cab driver and got out. He opened the official letter he had received the week before and confirmed the address. 1414 Washington was a towering, black windowed building over a hundred stories tall. The architect had deviated from the standard, flat top roof that dominated the downtown sky line and placed an arc on the top of this, making his building look like a large, black tombstone. The irony of placing the Department of Aging in this building was not lost on Gerald Stern.

His appointment was at three and he took the elevator to the 77th floor. He signed in on the computer kiosk and grabbed the last open chair in the middle of the crowded waiting room. He looked into the faces of the others, most of them were old and wrinkled like his, some spoke into cell phones, some read the paper like they were in a coffee shop, and still others looked at the ground or at their hands and no one made eye contact.

A large, L.E.D. reader board chimed every few minutes and a name flashed across the panel. Someone would stand and shuffle in or roll their wheel chairs to the hallway marked "ENTER," their seat to be quickly taken by a new arrival. Gerald kept checking his watch, three o'clock, three fifteen, three thirty, four o'clock, it really didn't matter, he had no place to go.

The chime rang four times in quick succession and he looked up and saw his name flashing on the screen. He stood slowly and made his way to the "ENTER" sign as someone took his seat. He entered the hallway and placed his right hand on the hand scanner and it read his palm, confirmed his identity and flashed the number 911. He walked down the long hall until he found office number 911 and knocked.

The door opened and a kid no older than twenty nine opened the door.

"Come in, come in, I'm Dr Weingarten," he said and shook Gerald's hand. "Please, have a seat," he said pointing to the overstuffed leather chair by the window. Gerald's bones ached and he eased himself into the low leather chair. He wondered how he would be able to stand after the interview. The doctor sat across from him in a matching chair, a glass coffee table between them. Gerald looked out the window with the view of the river; he saw small fishing vessels sailing out to sea and recalled his days on the water with his dad, and later with his wife Marie and even later his son, Jonathan.

"Well, how have you been Mr. Stern?" the doctor asked. "I see it has been 2 years since your last evaluation.

"Yes," Gerald said.

The doctor scanned through the think folder on his lap, pausing to study some pages, rapidly going through others and often rubbing the light stubble on his chin.

"It looks like your cholesterol is up a bit, over 200," the doctor said without looking up, "and you haven't done a good job controlling your blood sugar, mmm, in fact, it's all over, lows in the forties, highs in the 220's, not good Mr. Stern," he said, this time looking up.

Gerald was watching a sail boat catching the wind and racing out to sea. He owned a 22-footer like it years before and named it for his wife, the M.S. Beauty. Every weekend they would hit the bay and sail until time forced them back home and back into the daily grind. Jonathon gave up sailing for faster sports, cars and women and did little sailing after he turned sixteen. The wife's knees gave out and she couldn't help with the sails and complained about the pain the constantly shifting boat caused her knees. The boat was dry docked and later sold to pay for the surgery on her knees, her knees worked great but then there was nothing to sail.

"…and your blood pressure is much higher than before, are you taking you medicine? Ah, Mr. Stern, are you taking your medicine…for your blood pressure… it seems that it and your glucose are out of control and usually the meds…Mr. Stern, are you paying attention."

Gerald looked away from the window and the boat and stared at the little boy in front of him. He knew of nothing. He wore a white lab coat and tried to grow a goatee in an effort to look more doctorly, the image failed, he looked like a kid in his dad's lab jacket with an adolescent beard.

"Medicines? No, can't afford them," Gerald said and looked at the abstract paintings on the wall, the modern vase with artistic sticks protruding from them like dead wood.

"Now, Mr. Stern…do you mind if I call you Gerald? No? Good, now Gerald, you know your Medicare will cover all of your meds, even mail them to your house if you want, money is no object, but you must fill them and then you must take them."

"Yeah, I've been planning on it…"

"Mr. Stern, ah, Gerald the meds would…" he saw Gerald was staring out the window, lost in the water in the bay.

"It's your wife isn't it?" Weingarten said. "It's Marie, isn't it?"

Gerald's head turned toward the doctor quickly and his instinct wanted to pounce, but his legs would not support such an activity, so he just held the doctor in a stare.

"I don't mean to bring back painful memories, but I see you lost your wife two years ago, they retired her due to advanced metastasis of breast cancer."

"The damn quacks should have caught it for-Christ's-sake, it was only breast cancer," Gerald said.

"They usually do, looks like a problem with the mammography machine, poor contrast, they did recall that machine after 14 deaths, you did get a settlement."

"Damn the settlement, Marie shouldn't have died," Gerald said, his legs tense.

"No, she shouldn't have, but, unfortunately she did and that's when you quit taking care of yourself, Mr. Stern."

"What's the point?"

"You have a lot to live for Mr. Stern, your son Jonathon and his daughter, Mary-Sue, his wife."

"They don't come round much."

"He is a chemical engineer, looks like he travels a lot, but what about your painting, you were good at that, but I show nothing in your financial statements that shows any recent purchases of paint or canvass," Weingarten said, flipping through the file.

"No."

"Painting, sailing, golf, didn't you ever take up golf," he said, flipping pages in the file.

"No, not much sport in following a little ball around the grass."

"Ah, Mr. Stern, it's great fun. Let me see, your best friend, Carl, died last month of heart failure, sudden, I'm sorry."

"He was a good friend," he said and stared at his hands.

"Oh Mr. Stern, this is not looking good, no hobbies, no friends, no close family. I show a projected 40% increase in medical costs in the next 62 months with a potential of a minus six on quality of life, especially in light of your non-compliance," he said and made notes on a clip board.

"You don't want to be an invalid, a cardiac cripple or suffer debilitating paralysis from a stroke do you?"

"No," Gerald said.

"You know, the diabetes could cause you to go blind, lose your kidneys, you are showing a 33% chance of blindness in two years and possibly a kidney transplant in four if you do not get compliant." He paused and studied Gerald Stern's face and saw what he had seen frequently since taking this job. Hopelessness.

"Mr. Stern, you still have a substantial amount of money from the settlement, you could travel, you could go visit your grandchild. I see you have some college buddies in Santa Fe, Mark and Edgar, their friend depth is rapidly dwindling, you could reach out to them, it would greatly improve both of your life scores. "

"I don't want to travel, don't want to see friends I haven't seen in decades, hands hurt too much to paint, can't be too far from a shitter in case my bowels decide to blow, my bones hurt, can't remember shit, ain't nothing on the TV to watch, hell, even my damn dog died.

"Yes, I see Skipper was run over by a car last June, I'm sorry."

Gerald sat there and stared at him, glanced at his watch, looked out the window and saw the light was fading on the water.

"Mr. Stern, please, I need something, anything."

Gerald glared at him.

"Ok then, I'm sorry, Mr. Stern, I'm going to have to recommend permanent retirement sir…"

Gerald didn't say a thing, he knew the drill, he would be escorted to a cubicle where he would sign a stack of papers donating all his personal possessions to his remaining family and to the state to offset medical care and they would take him into a dark room, lay him on a gurney and inject a single medicine that would stop his heart, quickly and painlessly. He would get a write-up in the paper and a note would be sent to his remaining friends and family. He had received many such letters in the mail.

Dr. Weingarten pressed a button on his chair and three large men in green surgical scrub attire and long white lab coats entered. Gerald stood slowly and paused to watch the last ray of the sun sink behind the water and limped slowly out the door.

"Just one hope sir," he said as the door closed behind Gerald Stern, "that's all I needed was just one hope."

V

BIG BILLY BOGGUS'S
BESTEST JOB

Big Billy Boggus looked at the girl with the pimples and braces and asked her again, "Do you want fries with that?"

She just stared at him through thick, black framed glasses. "MMM, oh, well, ok," she said.

"Do you want French Fries, Curley Fries, Home-style fries or Tots?" Billy asked.

"Ah, mmm, well, I don't know, just fries I guess, no, make 'em Home-style," she said shifting from leg to leg.

"Do you want them plain, seasoned, spicy or flamed?" Billy said in a monotone.

"Plain," she said decisively.

"Would you like any toppings with that?"

"Like what?" she said, looking over Billy's shoulder at the French Fry pictures on the menu.

"Bacon bits, cheese, onions, peppers, ranch dressing, ketchup, spicy tomato sauce or cracked peppercorn?"

"Does that cost extra," she asked.

"Yes," Billy said.

"How much extra," she asked. Billy stared at her, looked behind her at the growing line of impatient lunchers.

"Which one?" he asked.

"Huh?"

"They each cost different," Billy said.

"Oh. I want cheese, bacon bits and ranch dressing," she said.

Billy punched her selection into the cash register. "That will be nine dollars and fifty two cents."

"What?"

"Nine dollars and fifty two cents," he said again.

"I don't have that much money," she said.

"We take MasterCard, Visa, American Express, Discover, Diners Club and Bucky Bucks."

"Do you take checks?"

"No."

"How much is it without the fries?"

Billy voided the transaction and input her hamburger and drink order without the fries. "That will be six dollars and eighteen cents."

"I only have five bucks," she said.

"Bucky Bucks or dollars?" he asked.

"Dollars."

Billy voided the latest transaction and rang up just a hamburger.

"It will be four dollars and nineteen cents for the hamburger."

"That doesn't come with a Coke."

"No."

"How much is water?"

"Dasani, Evian, Crystal Springs or tap."

"Tap."

"Tap is free."

"Can I have a glass of tap water then?"

"Small, medium, large or a Bucky Bucket?"

"It's all free?"

"Yeah."

"I'll take the Bucky Bucket."

Billy pulled her burger from beneath the heat lamp, stuck it in a sack, stuck a Bucky Bucket cup under the ice and water dispenser and waited. The lunch line stretched to the ketchup counter.

He put a lid on the water and gave the pimple faced girl her order and said, "Thank you for choosing Bucky Burgers for your fast food needs. Come again."

The next person in line had a hard time deciding between mustard, mayonnaise, ketchup or super sauce on her burger and the day droned on for hours.

Billy got home at four and went straight to the computer. He had twenty two emails. His mom opened the door still dressed in her night gown and a robe. "How was your day, Honey?" she said, a cigarette dangling from her mouth, cheap Scotch in her hand.

"Fine, Mom."

"That's good," she said and leaned over and kissed him on the cheek, she closed the door and shuffled back to her bedroom.

Billy answered emails from his friends, mostly gamers he met online. He was the master cracker of the gaming world. He had found the secret treasure door in Witch World within two days of release and found the flaws in Armageddon that allowed infinite lives. He had found flaws and hacked into all the latest games and he published the cheat codes on his blog.

He sat up till three a.m. playing Aqua Wars and fell asleep in his chair. The alarm woke him at 10 a.m. and he threw on a t-shirt and rushed to work without a shower. He fed the masses until four and returned home to answer email and pursue the demon fish king in Aqua Wars. By the third day the manager asked him to change his pants and shower, there had been complaints.

Billy beat Aqua Wars on the fourth day, a world record he was certain. He searched the web and downloaded a pirated copy of Sing Pow Pootie, a Japanese super-hero karate game that wasn't due out for another two weeks. He beat it before midnight and went to bed.

His cell phone woke him at 9 a.m. The number was blocked but he answered anyway.

"Hello?" he said.

"Is this Billy Boggus?"

"Yes."

"Are you the Billy Boggus of Boggus's Game Blog?"

"Yes."

"I'm Chrone Reed from Aderock Games."

Billy's felt his stomach do a somersault. He had just posted game breakers on his blog to their new game, Desert Devils.

"I, ah, what do you want?" he asked.

"We've been watching you Billy, you are quite quick at breaking our codes and posting them on your site," he said.

"I'm sorry, it's… ah…it's a hobby…" he stammered.

"It's ok Billy, if our codes are so simple that you or someone else can break them so quick, so we want you to show how to fix the flaws in all our games."

"You mean, you want me to go to work for you?" Billy said.

"You betcha Big Billy, we want you to come play our games, show us where they are weak and fix them for us," he said.

"That sounds like a lot of work," Billy said.

"No Billy, not at all, we would pay you to play video games all day and then, instead of telling the world on your blog, just tell us," he said.

"You mean I'd get paid to play video games all day?" Billy said.

"You bet," he said.

"Oh wow, I'd love to," Billy said.

"Good, come to the gate, I will send you a map, they will expecting you, we will pay you well and you can play all the games you want.

"When do I start?" Billy asked.

"Today, you start today," he said and hung up.

Billy showered and put on a his Valliant Victor Vector shirt with the cool ray gun and Victor Vector Car. He printed out a simple map that Crone had sent and rushed the ten miles to the gates. He pressed the button and a voice said "What?"

"I'm Billy Boggus, I'm expected," he said.

After a long minute the gates opened and he followed the signs to the main building. A tall, boney man with sharp features met him, he was pale, and wore a long white lab coat.

"Good, come," he said and led Billy to an elevator. He pressed the circled minus 9 and the elevator jerked and descended quickly. Chrone said nothing. When the doors opened he was hit with a blast of cold air and saw computer screens and wires and lighted diodes that covered every wall. They walked past several terminal stations where other young men sat staring intently on the games in front of them.

"Do they work here too?" Billy asked.

"Yes, they are your co-workers, they have each been assigned a game, like you will Billy."

They stopped at an empty station. Large, high definition monitors surround him, there were several joy-sticks, a keyboard, pointing devices and cables and wires that draped around the station like jungle snakes.

"This is your…place, you have been assigned Domino Dynamite."

"I've never heard of it," Billy said.

"Yes, it's top secret, brand new, Status Alpha, we have put a lot of capital into developing this game, we don't want the code cracked its first week out, so you must find its flaws and fix it first."

"Great," Billy said and sat down in the big padded chair, it fit him like a glove and he sank into the smooth leather. He heard the whirr of tiny motors as they adjusted to his position, filling in spaces to support and snuggle him. He chose the latest game hand set, the Electro glide 9000 Digital-heat sensing hand control that had no moving parts making it virtually unbreakable. He had read about it in the game mags but they were not yet available for retail sale.

Dominoes Dynamite was action packed and challenging, it required quick reflexes and some strategy and he found a big flaw in it during the first hour that made him indestructible for five minutes each time he jumped four dominoes in a set pattern. He pressed a big red button on his chair that marked the place on the game and recorded the pattern of his moves. He found three more quickly when a large pizza arrived by robotic cart. The steel cart rolled up and stopped by him and a lid opened, inside was a large double topped, thick crust, garlic butter pepperoni pizza and a two liter bottle of Coke with a large cup of ice. Billy gobbled it down and played until the computer froze.

Billy pushed buttons and twisted knobs and Chrone walked up and said, "you have done a great job today, Billy, time to go," he said.

"What, I don't want to go," Billy said.

"No, no, just for now, it's five o'clock, you get to go home, be back tomorrow, eight o'clock, ok?" Chrone said.

"Oh, ok," Billy said. He left and noticed everyone else had already gone. He got back in his car and went home. He ate a frozen pizza and played Battle Brigade until midnight. He woke at his computer screen at 7:30 in the morning, and rushed to work. He hadn't time to shower.

He sat at his station and played Domino Dynamite until the lunch robot brought tacos and a two liter Coke. He ate and played, marking mistakes along the way. The day went quick and when the computer froze, Billy climbed out of his chair and went home.

The next day he arose, washed his face and sprayed on some cologne, his pants were tight and he struggled to get in them. Outside, a blue van with 'Aderock Games' written on the side was waiting for him. A young man in a black suit opened the side door for him and Billy climbed in and he was chauffeured off to his job.

The van took him home that night and a large box was waiting for him on his bed. He opened it up and found it filled with t-shirts and sweat pants with logos and characters from Aderock Game company. Each day he climbed into the van and it took him to the door of the company, he rode a conveyor belt to his station and snuggled into a new chair and played games all day. The lunch robot brought him food each day and came around with soft drinks, energy drinks, candy and snacks all day.

They fixed the flaws he found each day in Domino Dynamite and he played it again the next day, trying to find more. He went days without finding any and finally found the game unbeatable. He tired of it and was going to say something to Chone the next day.

He got out of the van the next work day and hobbled to the elevator. He was winded when he got there, he had put on some pounds while working there. When the elevator doors opened, Chrone was waiting.

"You are doing well, yes?" he said.

"Yes, good…"

"Good, you have been promoted Billy, rather quickly I might add," he said.

"A promotion?" Billy said.

"Yes, new game, new floor, where only our best, most dedicated players play," he said.

Chrone pressed a button with a triangle on it and they descended well below the 9th floor. The doors opened they got off onto a dark corridor lined with doors and large, square windows. He saw other employees in private room playing games on neat, clean work stations. The rooms were bright, unlike the cubicle station he had been working at. The conveyor started up and carried them down to a room marked, 1113.

"Here we are Billy, your new home," he said and smiled.

Billy waddled through the door and into the big room. The console was very neat, no wires crisscrossed the workstation, there was only one large monitor in the center of the room and he saw the latest in game gear on a table next to the chair. He sat and felt the chair caress him like a glove. He settled in and played a new game, Gobi's Surprise, a role playing game about a small golden wood chuck in a fantasy realm. The lunch robot brought him pizza and Twinkies and a large chocolate malt. He sucked the ice cream through a straw and played on.

Chrone walked in to check on him and Billy said, "Chrone, this is the best job ever, I love it here," he said.

"Good," he said, "I'm so glad."

Billy squirmed in his chair, "I have to go to the bathroom, where is it?" Billy asked.

"Down the hall," he said and Billy waddled to a door marked 'Men.' Billy had trouble going through the door and turned sideways to squeeze through and struggled to get into the stall where he pulled his flab up on each side and sat on the toilet just in time for an explosive bowel movement. He felt pizza and tacos and chicken strips pouring from him, he couldn't reach to wipe his butt and waddled to the door. He turned sideways and tried to push himself through, he pushed and struggled and got stuck halfway through, he panted, held his breath and pushed harder and was lodged, his head got weary and he blacked out.

He awoke and was staring at a large, round light. Chrone stood over him and said "yes, yes, he's ok," he-he he laughed. "Congratulations Billy, you have been promoted to Master Gamer," he said, "yes." Billy smiled, "really?"

Two men in masks appeared over him and he heard a whooshing sound and felt immense pain in his rectum, he looked down and saw a wide, flexile tube being placed up his anus and felt suction pressure so intense he passed out again.

The images in front of him were blurry and the room swirled and came slowly into focus. He was in his chair, the big monitor in front of him. Chrone was standing at his side, "Good, you're awake I see, yes, good," he-he, "we were worried, yes, you have completed the transformation to Master Gamer Mr. Boggus, congratulations," he said.

Billy felt high. "Before you is our latest game, ten years in the making, Domino Dynamite II, see if you can beat it," he said and exited the room.

Billy began playing, it was real similar to DD I and he had long tired of that game. He adjusted in his chair, heard the motors whirr, tried to move his left leg to relieve the cramp in his calf and found his legs were gone, he was wearing a diaper and stubs stuck out from his body, covered in bloody bandages and a red tubes came from groin that went to a small bag half filled with dark, yellow urine, a wider tube stuck out of his stomach carrying solid waste and he saw another tube coming out of his neck with yellow/green fluid flowing in.

He realized he was being fed and he would never have to stop for a bathroom break, pause to eat, stop to pee, he began Domino Dynamite II, determined to beat the game in one day. He couldn't believe his luck. This was Billy Boggus's Bestest Job Ever!

VI

▼

THE OBLIQUITY OF
THE ECLIPTIC

Hector Eugene Bartholomew III fell off the earth at 12:09 pm, Eastern Standard Time. By all accounts he was the first. Eyewitnesses, whose accounts are often unreliable and usually unverifiable, seem to agree it was approximately 12:09 pm, 12:10, or 12:15 EST, but after this, their stories differ widely and often completely.

Some witnesses claim he suddenly disintegrated into dust and blew away like an ash. Some say lighting struck him, like the spear of God striking him dead and in a flash, he was gone. Others claim he simply exploded, *spontaneous evaporatous*, yet no one could explain what happened to the body parts or the large amount of blood that would have accompanied an anatomical explosion of a human being. No DNA evidence, neither blood, nor bone nor hair was found at the scene, fans of TV police forensic shows were quick to point out.

Amateur and professional meteorologists argue, correctly, that there were no clouds in the sky and no evidence of any electrical activity. There were no burn marks on the sidewalk and no thunder was heard by any of the witnesses, possibly ruling out a lighting strike but still leaving intact the Hand of God theory.

The most common recollection of said event was that Mr. Hector Eugene Bartholomew III shot up into the sky like a rocket. Witnesses here too differed on the details, some claiming they were burned by the propulsion exhaust that shot from the bottom of his feet, like a NASA shuttle launch, while others, and there were more of these who claimed that there was no heated exhaust plumage, but only a thin white vapor trail against the pale blue sky.

These varying accounts led some to believe, later denied by government officials, on and off the record that Mr. Hector Eugene Bartholomew III was a scientist or CIA operative, working on some super-top-secret Personal Propulsion Device, a so called PPD NBC was PDQ to claim they coined. Skeptics and conspiracy theorists argue that the government did, would and always will deny any and all such accusations of potential and actual paranormal events, and offer as irrefutable proof the government's continual denial the aliens found in Area 51. These arguments quickly descended into a quagmire of conflicting, fanatical and irrational conspiratorial theories that fed the lascivious appetites of those who loved to dine on lurid details.

The puzzling thing about this and all the other theoretical pinings of the masses and the accompanying hysteria was that only one person said anything to anybody about Mr. Hector Eugene Bartholomew III disappearance, until after his reported disappearance by his wife, and that was from the cigar man on the corner of Main who was accustomed to Mr. B's regular patronage when he left the office at lunch each day.

Of course, at least two witnesses claim it was aliens that abducted him in a sleek silver spaceship carried him away 1). on a great, wide tractor beam and 2). by a giant green tentacle. These two witnesses could not agree on the method of abduction, but did agree on 1). aliens, 2). sleek, silver spaceship and 3). a secret memory eraser beam was used to confuse them.

Another Sector of the Strange claimed, as they always do, looking for and almost hoping for the end of the world that it was a sign of the second coming of the good Lord Jesus Christ Almighty. They claimed, and there were several others who did so also, that a great light appeared above them and time stood still and the man floated into heaven like a saint. Friends and business associates of Mr. Hector Eugene Bartholomew III and even Mrs. Hector Eugene Bartholomew III, were quick to say, respectfully, that he was no saint and not even likable at times.

Gossipers and shameless Do-Gooders were quick to chirp in, at every media opportunity/man-on-the-street interview/YouTube documentary that, resulting from Hector Eugene Bartholomew III's questionable and deplorable lifestyle, which none knew any specific details about, but were quick to speculate on by expanding on Mrs. Hector Eugene Bartholomew III's claim that Mr. Hector Eugene Bartholomew III was "not a saint," and extrapolated to the Nth degree that he must, in fact be of questionable character and deserved to be gone from this earth.

The furor over Mr. Hector Eugene Bartholomew III questionable acts grew so fast that Mrs. Hector Eugene Bartholomew III was quickly sued by so-called victims of said questionable acts by people who had never met, never come in contact with nor had any relationship with, in person or otherwise with this "horrid little man," as one victim said. One later claimed that she was carrying his baby, in what would be the only second incident of immaculate conception in recorded history and contributed to the many conspiracy theories in such that Mrs. Hector Eugene Bartholomew III had to go into hiding and was unable to go public to defend her husband, who, although was not a saint, had been a good, god fearing, church-going man with the normal accumulation of bad habits and ill tempers as any other man of sixty-two and a success in accumulating decent sums of money. One paper printed a quote on page 9 of section 3 near the bottom beneath an orange juice ad that Mrs. Bartholomew had said the "Gene," as he was called, had been "a good provider for his family, and in over thirty-two years of marriage had never struck her, nor their children, was fair in business and tithed to the church," but other than the page nine, section three report, because of Mrs. Bartholomew's self imposed and forced exile, the dastardly rumors of Mr. Bartholomew's alleged indiscretions were allowed to spin wildly out of control and continued to be headliners in the daily papers for several days.

The accusations and insinuations may have continued indefinitely about Mr. Hector Eugene Bartholomew III and the Bartholomew Lady Immaculate of the unconfirmed conception had it not been for Fredrick Lawrence Johnson of Monte Sereno, California. He did not know, nor was ever known to be an associate of, nor associated with, Mr. Hector Eugene Bartholomew III, et al, but will be, forever attached to Mr. Bartholomew in the history blogs as the second known person to have disappeared, inexplicitly from the earth.

Like Mr. Bartholomew III, Mr. Johnson was reportedly walking down the street between the hamburger establishment in which he had just dined with close associates from the computer place he was employed, to the office where he would return to complete the remaining four hours of his day, making the time approximately 1 p.m. when, in front of his good friends and long term associates, he was sucked into space with not so much as a whoosh, a blast or even a vapor trail, said various witnesses, and there were several, both friendly and familiar with F.L. Johnson as well as independent witnesses who, thus far, have no ulterior motive to delude or deceive an increasingly concerned community. Like Mr. Bartholomew, Mr. Johnson was never seen or heard from again.

Like fanatics on the East Coast, fanatics on the West Coast, and there were many there too who fed and were nurtured by the main stream media by dreams of five minutes of fame and possible fortune, stated that they saw 1). Tentacles 2). a tractor beam, 3). a bright light, 4). silver, sleek, flying saucers, 5). The Mothman, (winged alien creatures previously found only in West Virginia and in some dilapidated drive-in movie theaters as the third feature), 6). and, as one homeless Catholic lady claimed, it was Jesus Christ himself, coming down on clouds to carry Mr. Johnson away and gave proof of the event by showing the beloved Virgin Mary's portrait on her toasted raisin bread.

But most witnesses, as was previously described as sensible and sane said he was simply pulled into space suddenly, no wind, no beams, no lights, no aliens, no tentacles, no giant holy hand, no lightning bolt or ground shaking thunder or super secret personal jettison devises. They said he was walking along, specifically next to Fred Nitameyer, telling one of his many bad jokes, which all his friends claim they had heard before but which the actual punch line escaped them at the time of the interview, when he simply shot into space. Looking up, Mr. Nitameyer said he saw his friend accelerate into the sky and wobble like balloon to a fro, the way a balloon careens slightly from side to side on the whims of the wind when it slips from a little boy's hand and is soon too small to see and is swallowed by the vastness of the sky. Mr. Johnson did not scream, did not shout and did not wave good bye. Some say it was not in his nature to cause a scene.

While there is little debate Mr. Bartholomew and Mr. Johnson were the first wide witnessed accounts of Sudden Human Disappearance Syndrome (SHDS), anther acronym created by and frequently adopted by various media outlets, there were of course, later, others who claimed to be the first and several who filed lawsuits against NASA, the CIA, the tobacco companies, Microsoft and others claiming that they had lost loved ones to SHDS. Still others sued and some attorneys sought class action status for suits related to the witnessing of SHDS which caused irrevocable shock, trauma and insomnia, although to who the lawyers would actually hold liable for these events was still in question. SHDTSS-Sudden Human Disappearance Traumatic Shock Syndrome got wildly popular with frequent sad stories on the news of those affected by the loss of a loved one and the traumatic stress of witnessing their sudden disappearances.

People were quick to seek legal advice on their rights and well being and who could be blamed for their losses and their general unease caused by these sudden disappearances and thus seek compensation for their issues. The number of potential plaintiffs as well as the list of potential defendants grew exponentially with each vanishment.

A newly elected Congressman from the state of Massachusetts proposed legislation extending various Medicare and Social Security benefits to victims of SHDTSS, but this effort was short lived as the Congressman became a victim of SHDS himself, disappearing in front of a home town crowd gathered on the square, in the middle of his speech, punching a hole in the garden gazebo named after him for his wonderful contributions to the city. Witnesses said he was shouting and pounding on the podium when he suddenly shot into space. Most people did not notice and finally looked up to see he was gone when the shouting stopped. Everyone made it home in time for dinner.

Reports came from all over the world about Sudden Human Disappearing Syndrome or simply Human Suddenly Disappearing, with most witnesses confirming the more reasonable accounts that the person was there one moment, and gone the next, simply racing into space, with no reports of space ships or tentacles or tractor beams being seen. This was later confirmed by a myriad of amateur photographers with digital cameras and camera cell phones as well as professional photographers, journalists, artists, and news videographers who captured the expulsions on video tape, film microprocessors and even canvas with colorful paints and oils.

Satellite images, passenger airlines and military reconnaissance aircrafts reported that these individuals were indeed launching into space, suddenly expelled into the atmosphere and shooting well beyond the reach of gravity. The space shuttle Nutation II was launched into orbit to observe this phenomenon. Their reports were TOP SECRET and highly classified and the images and radio traffic between the shuttle and space agency headquarters were electronically scrambled and top-secretly coded by the best minds and computers the government had to offer, but non-the-less, these images and transmissions were quickly hacked and soon appeared on You-Tube and Yahoo's most "Frequently E-mailed Stories" section. The raw footage showed people floating peacefully in space in a large, black ocean, their arms and legs swaying slightly as if swimming in a placid sea. They bobbed and bumped into each other in a gravity free soup. Some wore business suits or jogging pants and some were naked as if plucked from the shower.

The images were at first disturbing until someone set the pictures to a sound track by the latest girl band from Britain and circulated as a music video on the internet. These deep space dancers, set to music, made the video so popular and the CD sell off the charts so quickly that the previously unknown girl band's first and only album went Super-Quadruple Neon Platinum in the first week alone. Of course, the lawsuits soon started, as families and friends objected to seeing the caricatured corpses of loved ones gyrate to a pop love song, but the unfettered nature of the internet made precise placement and blame and thus responsibility and liability for supposed malfeasance impossible.

Typically the news, at five-six and ten p.m. as well as five-seven-eight a.m. and once at noon and every hour on the hour on such stations as CNN, HNN, FXN and MSNBC (until replaced briefly by reports of the President's gall bladder operation), reported dire accounts of the increasing number of sudden planetary departures or SPD's.

But the fate of these Exiteurs, as ABC states they labeled first, was largely unknown prior to the shuttles footage. By this time, thousands of people, and a large number of large animals, primarily horses, cows, elephants, rhinos and the occasional large goat, were reported to have launched and left the earth. From space the pictures were spectacular, a spate of tiny bodies shooting like rockets into space, some to travel through the atmosphere and survive the tenacious grip of gravity to wind up on the British Babe's video, but most became human torches, a flux of fireworks as bodies tore through space and burst like flowers in the sky. Spectators on the earth said the exhibition was outstanding and sale of telescopes rose one-hundred and fifty-two percent. Young lovers flocked to places like Lover's Leap, Love's Lookout and the Point to neck romantically on old blankets and watch the nightly fireworks. Teen pregnancy increased by 20 percent.

It created an ethical and moral dilemma as many wrestled with the yin and yang of life. At once the display of exploding humans resembled a beautiful shower of shooting stars in the sky but the fodder for the show was people. The syndrome created by the psychological conflict is being discussed by psychologists and various governmental committees and an appropriate label is due out by November, if all parties can agree.

Despite the nightly fireworks display, the world, as a whole became depressed. People in many religions accepted the fact of life and death and life in the here-after or a return ticket to earth as another being, a cockroach or a king, depending on one's outlook on life and fate and supreme deities, and people, regardless of religion or lack thereof, understand, although may not agree with, the randomness of existence and the finiteness of life.

That notwithstanding, the certain uncertainty that permeated gave more credence to the old saying, "Here today, gone tomorrow" with increased urgency and unpredictability of the "GONE" part. People exited the earth in mid-sentence, mid-stride, mid-stroke, just as they would in death, but this was something more, more random, more immediate. There was no time to contemplate, to speculate, to pontificate or grieve. No time to get one's affairs in order, to write love letters or last wills and testaments, to turn off stoves or close doors, to converse with attorneys or medical specialists to surmount a bona fide attack/defense against filcher vital.

This invisible hand, this cosmic robber stole young and old, frail and fit, rich and poor, known and the imperceptible from markets and malls, dinettes and dinners, ceremonies and bathtubs, from crowded streets to those standing in showers, naked and alone. There were no laws to control it, no denials to confound it, no scientists to explain it, no preachings that would comfort; it was all too unexplainable, too immediate and increasingly all too prevalent. The people of the world quaked on stilted legs and tried to continue on as if nothing were unusual.

The numbers increased, hundreds, then thousands a day, spread out in country to country, state to state, city to village to borough, human projectiles shooting into the sky in rapid succession like Armageddon.

Airlines reported people shooting past the wings, like missiles, and as the number of projectiles increased and people crashed against the wings, air travel was restricted. People crashed through buildings and cars, pulled from their couches and through the roofs into space, leaving large holes and dismayed families, their ceilings open to rain and wind. Some stood beneath the newly created hole in their homes and watched the fireworks created by their family members.

The world attempted to continue, to ignore the common occurrences. It was a battle against chaos, an attempt at normality, in a world without explanations. And it worked to some degree. No one was immune, no one could escape, no individual or group was excluded and therefore, for once, the world was equal. For life to continue, if the CEO suddenly became AWOL, the COO or CFO would simply step into the continuum and others stepped up to fill their positions as the business of business had to continue.

Meetings would progress, commerce would be made, decisions would evolve and the speaker would disappear, suddenly and without ceremony, and they would all pause, suck in their surprise and pause for a bit of mourning, and then the backup speaker would step in to continue on, as not to interrupt life for those remaining.

There were no phone calls from God, no explanations to the enlightened, and the world continued to turn. Some felt, they said, could feel the earth quiver under foot, a slight arrhythmia to the orbit, a hesitation of the spin, an alteration in the obliquity of earth's ecliptic, a groan felt from deep beneath the crust followed by a spectacular display of skylight flowers as thousands of people were tossed into space. The world would pause and look in awe at the fireworks and go about the business of existence, smiling but terrified that the next tremor would send them hurling into the clouds.

Back in the U.S., the cycle of life continued. In a mid-town hospital, a family gathered around a big panel window, and stared into the sterile environs of the nursery at the new arrival, a baby girl.

Elsewhere, halfway around the globe, beneath a grass thatched roof, in a tiny hut beside a stream, a woman without riches cried out in an empty village and bore down, pushing arduously with uterine muscles until the life inside her popped out. She knew the people of the village had all left in a fiery assent to Heaven, and she too would one day follow, but at that moment, she held her baby close and smiled as the tiny lungs inflated and let out a loud and healthy cry.

And in that instant, in New York City, near the same intersection, where Mr. Hector Eugene Bartholomew III became the earth's first Exiteur, another man, of unknown age or consequence, and with nobody to pause or notice, suddenly shot into the sky and exploded like a fire flower beneath a crescent moon.

VII

▼

SHOWER NOISE

Sandra checked the latches on the door, turned the deadbolt to the right, made sure the chain lock was secure. She peeked out the back window, peered into the corners of the drive, made sure no one was hiding in the shadows or ducked behind her car. She quickly opened the back door, set the hook locks on the screen and slammed the door shut and turned the dead bolt key to secure the lock, turned the door lock on the knob and finally wedged a bar stool behind the knob to secure it even more. She pulled the curtains tight and checked each room to be sure the blinds were closed, the living room, the tiny kitchen, the empty bedroom, her bedroom brightly lit and decorated in yellow flowers and lace.

Her home was now secure, there had been burglaries in the neighborhood and she was terrified of intruders. She had once been raped by a crack head who found her front door open and inviting, and she asleep on the couch. She didn't have much to steal, but what she had was hers and she had worked hard to get it.

Monday started out bad, she had been late to work, had not heard the buzzer on her alarm go off at 6 a.m., had gotten to the fabric store thirty minutes late and the owner, Mrs. Johnson was upset she actually had to wait on customers for half an hour before she arrived and had ignored her. She spent the long day listening to stories of arthritis, spoiled grand kids, dead husbands good and bad, of people she did not know that had recently passed, of grand trips she could never even dream of taking. She smiled and nodded and cut fabric all day knowing few panels would ever be made into dresses or blouses or quilts. Most would sit folded up in sewing baskets beside the patterns they were to be.

Mrs. Johnson left for lunch and never came back and Sandra worked the store alone till close. She sipped hot tea and ate some crackers and closed the shop at six. There was a chill in the air as the light faded. She stopped at the store and got some soup, a tin of cat food and a peach.

She scanned the neighborhood as she drove home, looking for strangers or anything amiss. She passed the Littleton home, it had been burglarized two nights before, thieves took the TV and the silver and Mrs. Littleton's wedding band.

Sandra turned into the drive of her tiny, vine covered A-frame. When she had bought it, it was cheap and small, but as the neighborhood had been reborn, her house became quaint and charming, she preferred the tax rate on the cheap and small house before it became fashionable.

The house secure, she fed the cat and heated the soup and sat in the quiet and ate. A few cars drove down the street, but none stopped. She had pictures of her kids above the television, Lilly when she was three, Violet at sixteen, Tom, at two before he died. She finished the soup and sliced the peach into tiny quarters and ate it slowly. It was nearing eight.

She washed the dishes in the sink and set them on the cupboard to dry. She checked the locks again and took her robe into the bathroom and locked the door behind her. She turned on the hot water until it was steamy and then mixed the cold until it was tolerable and stepped into the steamy shower. She let the jets of water rush all over her, let the water wash away the grime of the day, she bent her head beneath the stream and inhaled the steam into her lungs and washed Mrs. Johnson and her accusatory stares away, let the water carry the stories of widows and illness down the drain.

In the background she heard the phone, its steady rhythmic ring calling her, someone calling her, wanting her to answer. She stepped out and wrapped herself in a towel and padded down the hall to the kitchen phone, which of course had quit ringing. She looked at the caller ID and saw no new numbers. The TV was off, as usual. She must have been hearing things she thought and returned to the spraying streams of steamy water.

She locked the bathroom door and climbed in and winced as the hot water hit her skin and she readjusted to the heat, she soaped her body and washed her hair. She put Noxzema on her face when she heard the phone again and this time hurried to answer. She wrapped the towel around her and padded into the kitchen, the white cold cream still splotched across her cheeks and forehead. The phone sat silent and no evidence of someone calling.

She returned to the shower wondering. Could it be Lilly or Violet calling? Was something wrong with Mrs. Johnson? Probably an insurance salesman or someone selling tickets to the circus for crippled kids. Her kids seldom called. She washed the cold cream from her face and watched it swirl down the drain and rinsed all the soap from her body.

"Help me," she heard. Someone said softly, "help me," it sounded in the next room, drowned out by the sound of the shower. Someone was in her house.

She stood frozen in the shower, listening, turned the water quickly off, listened for a voice above the dripping of the shower head. Silence. She wrapped the towel around her and grabbed the toilet plunger as a weapon. She peeked out the door, listening intently, looking for movement and crept down the hall. She checked the doors, the locks, the windows; she peeked outside and up and down the deserted street. The phone sat silent. A chill climbed up her spine and she returned to the bathroom, left the door open and got dressed in her cotton night gown. She lay in bed and stared at the ceiling for hours before her mind slowed down and she could finally sleep.

The next day at the fabric store was like the others, Mrs. Johnson was off on Tuesdays and her daughter in-law filled in. Lorelei was fat and lazy and didn't have the aptitude to cut fabric straight. Customers complained and Sandra usually had to do all the cutting and her hands ached by the end of the day. She went home tired, ate her soup in silence, fed the cat and looked forward to her shower. The heat relaxed her hands and shoulders after a hard day like today, like every Tuesday.

She turned the shower on to hot and let the mirror fog before adding the cold water. The house was secure, she had seen to that, so she left the bathroom door ajar in case the phone rang again and climbed into the shower and let the burning water wash her day away. She had lathered up her hair when the phone rang again. This time she was certain. She wiped the raspberry suds from her eyes and rushed down the hallway with the bath towel flopping loosely around her. The phone stopped ringing as soon as she was close, she picked it up and heard the dial tone. She set the phone back on the cradle.

She glanced around the house, nothing out of place and she returned to the shower. This time she just sat on the edge of the tub and listened, she felt the soap drying in her hair and finally stepped in to wash the shampoo from her hair. Then she heard the voices, someone calling out, someone in the next room. She turned the water off and waited, the voices trailed away as the dripping water slowly stopped. Large droplets fell occasionally from the shower head like distant footsteps.

Sandra went to bed half wet and pulled the blankets tight around her and listened in the darkness for the sound of any strangers.

Wednesday, Sandra worked late. A supply truck came late, leaving boxes of patterns and needles and spools of thread and bolts of seasonal fabric. Sandra volunteered to stay late and stock the store and finished before nine. She drove home and went right to bed, too tired to shower she told herself.

She felt grungy at work all day Thursday, her hair was a mess and her hands still showed traces of dirt and dust from the day before. Mrs. Johnson seemed to notice but said nothing. She went home and baked a frozen pot pie, rocked in her chair for thirty minutes until the timer chimed. The chicken pie was still frozen in the center but the outside was warm and flakey and creamy gravy warmed her up. She gave the leftovers to the cat.

She felt the grime of two days work covering her body, two days of customers and Mrs. Johnson caked all over her. She took the telephone off the hook and turned the water onto hot, let the steam fill the bathroom and then turned on the cold. She stepped in and let the warm water run all over her, when she heard the phone ringing, rapidly, urgently calling her to answer. She climbed out and rushed naked down the hallway and stopped at the door. The phone was off the hook. The phone was on the counter, she picked up the phone and it was silent. She pressed the button on the receiver and then released it, she heard the dial tone beep. She set the phone back on the counter and returned to the shower, she needed more time beneath the water. The voices started immediately.

"Help us," it called, several voices, deep and swirling. "Help us," they pleaded from nowhere, from everywhere.

"Where are you?"Sandra called.

"Help us, please," the voices cried. "We're here," they said.

"I can't hear you very well," Sandra said and turned the water off and the voices stopped abruptly.

"Hello! Is anybody there?" she said; she only heard the water dripping in the tub. She turned the water on again, watched the swirling steam fill the room, the water splash on her skin, the water is much too hot but she hears the voices again, distant, calling, the mist takes shape or seems to form a face she has never seen.

"Is that you Tom?" she asked but got no answers.

She stood in the shower letting the water splash across her naked body, listened to the changing music of the water droplets on the wall and shower floor. She moved her body like a conductor, changing the distance the water traveled to her skin, moving again to change the distance that the water fell, the distance changed the pitch and the music that it made. The shower music and the steam erased the memory of the day until she heard the screams, of something far away, crying, calling, wailing.

She stepped once more outside the shower and listened quite intently. Hearing nothing she stepped out and turned the water off and listened more but again heard nothing. Walking out into the hall there was only silence, a car passing down the street, a dog barking far away.

Each night she lingered longer in the shower, listening to their cries, wanting to know the voices, voices that immediately depart when the water is shut off. Today had been a bad day; Mrs. Johnson had been a real bitch.

She felt the water on her back, the warmth run round her shoulders, felt the water swell around her breasts, cup them gently and when she feels the water squeeze she screams and hears a big splash of water by her feet, her lover leaves her quickly as the droplet fell.

Another day, another 8 hours of cutting fabric for old ladies who spend their days alone with dress patterns and sewing kits. There is so much more to life than making dresses.

On Friday, she rushed home and skipped her meal, jump naked into the shower and waited for the voices, waited for the caress of her lover. She heard their distant whispers, their woeful shouts, the desperate cries between the shower noise and then feels his presence there, her ghost lover in the water, she felt him cup her breast and press his firmness against her from behind, his watery caress brush across her neck.

And in the morning Sandra was gone, the shower still running, cold, the warm water used up long before. The police found Sandra's nightgown on the floor still wet. Mrs. Johnson was quite furious the next day when Sandra did not show up for work and she has to stay and work all day. She is unconcerned when the police arrive and she tells them how unreliable she was, "she'll turn up," she said and went back to cutting fabric.

That night, Mrs. Johnson got home tired, her hands hurt from cutting fabric all day. She sips her tea and a bowl of tomato soup. She takes her flannel jamas to the shower. She turns the hot water on slowly, feels the heat increase and mixes in the cold to get the temperature just right. She steps in and lets the water wash away the day and in the distance, as if just outside her door she hears the distant voices, hears the desperate cries of someone feeling pain.

Far away, she heard a voice she though she knew.

"Sandra, is that you?" she asked as the face appeared in the steam, caressed her face and pulled her down into the drain.

VIII

▼

LARAMIE

The sign said "Welcome to Laramie." Cleveland shook his head and rubbed the clouds from his eyes. Laramie? Where the Hell is Laramie? He was lying beneath the weathered sign, the letters hand painted on old planks in white. He rubbed his head, his mouth was dry, his eyes were still fogged by sleep. He lay upon soft dirt that swirled in the gentle breeze and tried to figure out where he was. He rubbed the back of his head and felt a large bump. He did not know where he was now, nor exactly where he was before, he only knew this had not been in his plans.

The dirt road stretched behind him and quickly disappeared into a thicket of tall, dark trees beyond the bend. Ahead of him, beyond the sign he saw two rows of buildings that made up the town of Laramie. Behind the town the trees faded into a shadow that ringed the tiny town.

He stood and walked towards town, the sunlight fading fast. He felt a cool wind blow behind him. Laramie looked like a ghost town from an old Western movie, cracked brown slat-board buildings, dark brown and weathered, marked with painted signs stating "General Store," "Hotel," "Stables," "Gunsmith," "Game Room-Free Pool" said another but there were no lights on and boards covered the windows. The only building with a light on was "Saloon," and he could see light coming through the swinging doors. There were no electric or telephone poles, no cars, no sounds of a highway, but overhead he saw a galaxy of stars pouring forth as the daylight faded. Millions upon millions of stars like he had never seen before.

From inside the saloon, he heard a player piano and boisterous laughter from a crowd. He stepped onto the porch and heard the loud thud of his dress shoes on the planks. The voices hushed a bit and he stood like an outlaw outside the swinging doors and peered in and let his eyes adjust to the light. It was an 1800's style saloon, a long, elegant wood bar, a mirror that ran the full length of the counter top, in the middle, a large, flat screen monitor showing a picture of a pendulum clock, a staircase leading upstairs to doors marked with single digits, thick red curtains, a life-size painting of a lady showing her knees beneath a ruffled petticoat, a smattering of patrons not dressed as from a movie of this time, but in a variety of clothes, a lady in a business dress, a farmer in a straw hat, a postman, a man in a suit, a Mexican cowboy in a big sombrero sporting a thick black mustache, two drug store cowboys with creased jeans and clean, white straw hats, a biker in black leather pants and sleeveless vest showing large, muscular arms covered in colorful tattoos, a young blonde woman in tight jeans, white t-shirt and a leather sleeveless vest, her red lips curled into a wicked grin, the lady from the painting, a young kid in khakis and long sleeved striped shirt sat at the piano, playing wildly and enjoying himself, a fat waitress in a stained t-shirt carrying a tray of glasses.

He entered and the music stopped, they all turned to stare, one man tipped his beer mug at him and then they all continued their conversations. The biker girl stared and smiled, the biker noticed. The music continued. He walked up to the bar. The bartender, wearing black pants and a red and white striped shirt and black hair slicked back walked up to him and asked, "what'll ya have?"

"I don't know," he said.

"How about a beer?" the bartender asked.

"Ah, I don't know if I have any money," he said and reached in his pocket for his wallet, it was gone, he began frantically checking his pockets.

"Ya don't need any money here, friend," he said and poured a dark draft with a thick head of foam on it.

He took the mug and gulped the brew down fast, it was lukewarm, but wet and it washed the dust down his throat. He wiped the foam from his lip and looked around the room. He noticed flat screen televisions in every corner showing old black and white movies, he saw John Wayne, Jimmy Stewart, Vincent Price, James Cagney, Humphrey Bogart and others in glamorous tones of black and gray. He finished his beer and turned to ask for another and found one already poured and waiting. He picked it up and sipped more slowly this time. He looked at his reflection in the mirror and wondered at the face that starred back. The face, familiar but nameless looked back, dark hair tossed and windblown, a sharp nose and age crevices along his cheeks, a long chin, handsome and gaunt. He wore a black tuxedo and a frilly white shirt, the bow-tie, untied, dangled around his neck, his collar open. He looked down and saw the brown dust that covered his black pants.

He looked into the mirror and saw the lady from the painting approaching him from behind. He turned and saw she was older now than when she sat for her portrait, her beauty had faded some and she tried to cover it with thick makeup that made her look more ghoulish than fresh.

"Hi, I'm Jane," she said and stretched her hand out for him to shake. He took her soft hand in his and shook it.

"Hi, I'm…ah, I'm…" he stuttered, unsure of who he was.

"Why Trent Smith, you don't need no introduction, we've all been expectin' you. Welcome to Laramie," she said and gave him a quick hug. The name seemed right, seemed familiar, seemed to fit so didn't offer any argument.

The bartender set a glass of champagne in front of her and she picked the tulip glass up with delicate fingers.

"Everybody," she said loudly and the room quickly hushed, "this is Trent Smith, he's the one we all been expectin' and my sighs if he ain't here." She raised her glass and everyone in the room lifted up their drink and toasted him.

"To Trent," they all said and went back to their thing, the people at the card table resumed play, the piano broke into another "JITTERBUG" tune. Several people stood and made their way over to him, including the biker chick.

"Hi, I'm Tom, Tom Jones, life insurance not internationally known pop singer," he said and offered his hand. He was a big man, with large hands and a dark, pin-striped suit. He wore a thick, gold watch on one wrist and a heavy, gold bracelet on the other. He was young but balding, he moved like an athlete but age and an increasing mid-section had slowed him down. The bar-tender passed Tom a beer.

The blonde in black leathers approached, "Hi," she said, her voice was thick and her words slightly slurred, "I'm Trinket," she said and hugged him. The biker guy walked up and pulled his girlfriend off, "I'm Big Mike," he said and grabbed his hand and squeezed, "you'll have to excuse her, she gets a little friendly when she's been drinking."

"Which is all the time," said Jane.

Big Mike quickly let go and took the beer the bar tender offered. He gently grabbed Trinket by the neck and led her back to the table.

A parade of people introduced themselves, the Mexican said hello in a heavy accent, the two cowboys, which he figured out quickly were gay, the woman in the pant suit who was quite drunk, all seemed very glad to see him.

The TV's in the corners, which had played old movies in silence suddenly switched to the bright and vibrant colors of the downtown parade, showing giant cartoon balloons and high school bands, soldiers dressed in sharp creased uniforms twirling their field weapons in a blur. The sound of marching bands blared through the speakers, drowning out conversations and the tune the piano player played. He jumped up, closed the lid and walked up and shook Trent's hand, mouthed the word "hello," and grabbed a beer from the bar.

Everybody stood and headed for the swinging doors and went out into the street. Jane grabbed his arm and squeezed and pulled him towards the door, he downed his beer and set it down on a table and walked out the doors, into the street. Main street was lit with bright, bare bulbs that hung by wires across the street. Every lamplight between every building was on, every light in every store was on, the windows rimed with multi-colored chasing lights ran in counter-clockwise circles. Brightly colored balloons were tied to all the hitching posts in front of every store, red, blue, green, yellow, pink, orange and purple balloons swayed gently in the evening breeze. The all linked arms and Trent was gently dragged toward the building marked "Good Eats." They all walked beneath a sign stretched across the street that said, "WELCOME TRENT."

They entered the restaurant crowded with small tables with white table clothes and four chairs each. The lights were warm and a heavy-set woman in a clean white blouse and checkered apron met them at the door, they all called her Mia. She approached him and welcomed him with a big smile. She stood by an open door and invited everyone inside.

In the back, on long, red-clothed tables was a succulent buffet, salad table spread with fresh fruits and toppings, nuts, dressings, pickles and olives and more at one, steamed ears of corn, squash, honey baked carrots, almond flaked beans, new potatoes with chives and sour cream, fat baked potatoes rolled in rock salt; the meat table was filled with plates of steak, ham, fried fish, steamed crab, broiled tuna steaks and more. There was a table of fresh baked breads and tubs of different butters and lastly the desert table filled with fresh cakes and warm pies and chocolate chip cookies the size of saucers. Mia placed a large plate in his hand and said "eat, then eat some more." More seemed the word of the day. He followed the line and people piled his plate high with food.

Mia led him to the table chatting up about how glad she was he was here, that she usually served three meals a day, sometimes more, snacks, formals dinners and buffets and that he hoped he would enjoy the food. The food looked delicious and he was starving. She sat him at the table with the postman, the farmer and the lady in the pant suit.

"Hi, I'm Larry," the postman said and extended his hand. Trent shook it.

"I'm Jed," said the farmer, clasping a thick ear of corn, he looked up and smiled but didn't offer to shake hands.

"I'm Elizabeth," said the lady in the pant suit and held her hand out and shook his, holding on a little long.

Trent dug into the food, every bite was a delight, fresh, tasty and warm. They ate in silence while Trent gorged to chase away the hunger.

"So Trent, where you from?" Jed asked.

"I...I don't remember," he said.

"What's the last thing you do remember?" Larry asked.

Trent paused a moment and thought. He had been at a party, he remembered champagne and city lights.

"I don't know. I was at a party, I remember drinking lots of champagne on the rooftop of a large suite, overlooking the city. "

"What city," Elizabeth asked.

"I don't remember. I can see familiar faces at the party, all dressed in formal ware, tuxedos, evening gowns, white gloved servants. I see the face of a woman, long green dress and shoulder length brown hair, beautiful, she is very close and I feel we were together."

"What else do you remember?" Larry asked. "Before or after that."

Trent paused and thought and tried to recall anything and couldn't. He sat there with a puzzled look on his face that made Elizabeth laugh and Trent looked up, Larry and Jed were smiling.

"What's so funny?" Trent asked.

"The look on your face, it's priceless," said Elizabeth.

"It's the same look we all get," Larry said.

"Can't remember nothin', can you," said Jed.

"No...no, I can't remember anything. I have images of the party, but no recall of where or why or who those people were. I can see them and then I woke up outside of town."

"And before that?" Larry asked.

"Before that, I can't remember anything, what I did for a living. Where I went to school, if I went to school, if I was married..." He looked down at his hands, there were no rings nor impressions or tan lines that he ever had any.

"Yep, same as all of us," Jed said, he'd finished his food and pushed his plate away, he was picking at his teeth with a toothpick.

"What?"

"It's the same for all of us," Elizabeth said. "We all woke up outside of town, under that sign, no recollection of where we were, or how we got here. Larry at least knows he was a postman."

"Last thing I remember was running from a big, red dog down the center of a street, running past small houses with chain link fences around the front yard."

"Last thing I remember was sitting on a tractor, mowing, smell of cattle all around me," said Jed.

"I was at some swanky bar, dark, smoky, nouveau art décor," said Elizabeth, "my finger stirring Scotch and rocks in a glass."

"Where is this place?" Trent asked.

"This is Laramie," said Jane. She walked up and placed her hands on Larry's and Jed's shoulders.

"But where, what state?" asked Trent.

"State of confusion," said Tom Jones the insurance salesman walking up, his large hands wrapped around a turkey leg.

Jane said, "we don't know, nobody does, it's just Laramie. Nobody can remember anything other than the last thing they did and waking up under the sign outside of town."

"We all saw the look," Tom said and smiled.

"We call it the Laramie stare," said Larry, laughing.

"What he means is the look new people get on their face when they try to recall their past, their last act and can't, that look of confusion and realization that they can't remember shit," Jane said.

"Are we dead?" Trent asked.

Jane laughed, "Oh no Honey, you're perfectly alive," she held out her wrist to him, "feel my pulse," she said.

"Feel my hands," Elizabeth said and touched his arm, "see, I'm warm," and looked into his eyes.

"So, we're not dead, is this like Purgatory," Trent asked.

"Sign said Laramie, didn't it?" said Jed.

"Yes."

"So, this must be Laramie," Jed said.

"I think people in Purgatory are already dead, they just stuck between the pearly gates and the roasting pit," said Tom, his turkey leg bare bone now.

"So what do we do here?" Trent asked.

"Do?" Elizabeth asked.

"Yes, what do you do all day here?" he said.

"Well, we eat, sleep, play cards," Jane said.

"We drink," said Elizabeth.

"We watch old movies, there's a bowling alley, an archery range, puzzles, crafts, a music store," said Larry.

"Do you play an instrument?" Jed asked.

"No," Trent said, Jed looked disappointed.

"Jed plays a mean banjo," Larry said.

"I mean, does anybody work?" Trent asked.

"Work, what for?" said Tom, he'd gotten another turkey leg.

"Who cleans, washes dishes, delivers the food and supplies?" Trent said.

They all stood silent with a blank look on their faces.

"I mean, Mia cooks, right?" he asked.

"No, Mia doesn't cook, she plays cards like the rest of us, she just likes to dress up in the apron," Larry said.

"The food's already laid out when she gets here, she just likes to greet people and make them feel at home," Jane said.

"Southern hospitality," Elizabeth said.

"The last thing she remembers was being in a large kitchen standing over a stove, so she thinks she was a cook or a chef," said Larry.

"Who's in the kitchen?"

"We don't know?" said Tom.

"I mean, through that door, marked kitchen, someone has to cook, don't they?" Trent said.

"We don't know, doors locked," said Larry, "it's always locked. We come here when it's time, foods hot and ready, we leave, we come back, everything's been cleaned up and the next meal is here waiting for us," Tom said.

"And your clothes? Who washes your clothes?" Trent asked.

"Same people that clean our rooms we guess," Jed said.

"What?"

"He don't get it," Jed said and got up and walked off.

"Honey, we don't know, we all woke up here, same as you, no memories, just our names. The food is prepared when we're hungry, our rooms are cleaned when we go back to our room," Jane said.

"There will be a clean tux in your room in the morning when you get up, your old one will gone," Tom said.

"There's always toothpaste and soap in the rooms, new puzzles on the shelf, the movies run continually," Larry said.

"If you use something, it's replaced the next morning," Tom said, licking his fat fingers.

"We just try to stagger our usage a bit," Jane said.

"The store only holds so much stuff," Larry said.

"Why don't you take extra?" Trent asked.

"Oh, you can't do that, can't be greedy, you can only have what you need, if you take more, it'll disappear," Jane said.

"Sometimes just the extra, sometimes all of it and you might have to wait a day or more to restock," said Larry.

"I took two tubes of toothpaste up to my room one time and the next day, one was gone, same as the next day and the day after, I'd go to the store and take extra toothpaste and each day, the extras would be gone. So I gets smart and the next day I take three tubes and hid them and the next day, all the tooth paste is gone," Tom said. "Every tube from everybody's room is gone, none in the store. Next day, everybody has a fresh tube and the store is stocked again. Lesson learned."

"Except one time, Elizabeth there took two bottles of Scotch up to Room 4 and they took away all our liquor for two days," Jane said.

"Who is they?" Trent asked.

"We don't know," Jane said, "They, them, whoever takes care of us here."

"You never see anybody, no cleaning people, no delivery people, no cooks, stockers?" Trent asked.

"No, we never see anybody, just us 'town folk' as we like to call ourselves," Jane said.

Trent noticed the lights in the café were fading, he looked around. Jane said it was time to go and they all filed out into the street and returned to the saloon, the player piano was already blaring. They all drank and laughed and he remembered standing around the piano and singing.

Trent woke the next day, sun streaming in from the window. He was lying on a small feather bed and lying next to Elizabeth. She was snoring loudly and her back was to him, her hair tangled and messed. He slipped quietly out of bed and found a fresh tux hanging in the closet. He dressed quietly and went out the door. He saw he was on the second floor of the saloon, overlooking the bar. He closed the door to Room 4 and went downstairs. The bar was empty. He went outside, into the glare of the sun.

The sun was high and bright, the colored balloons lay shriveled on the ground like spent condoms. He made his way toward the café and found it crowded with everybody, the 'town folk' as Jane had said. Boxes of day old donuts sat on the tables, he took two and went to the coffee pot and poured a cup and sat down with Jane, Trinket and Big Mike.

"Morning," he said glancing around. They each just smiled.

He bit into a donut, it was dry and stale, the coffee was cold. Everyone glanced up at him and then quickly away.

"What's up with everyone? He asked.

Big Mike looked at him and said, "Room 4."

"What?" Trent asked.

"You went up to Room 4 with that woman," Jane said.

"I don't remember anything," he said.

"Yeah, well, don't let it happen again, next time it'll worse than stale donuts," Mike said and got up, leaving a plate of stale donuts behind.

Lunch was much better, cold cut sandwiches and lemonade, dinner even better. Elizabeth ignored him all day.

Trent spent the next week exploring the town's shops, going to the movies, bowling. He found a driving range at the south end of town, complete with clubs and balls. The others claimed they never knew it was there. He found classic novels in the library, sketch pencils and pads in the craft shop, a very nice set of Ping clubs he used to work on his drive. They spent the daytime on individual activities and after a nice dinner would spend the evenings playing cards and drinking until retiring to their rooms.

The days droned on, there were no clocks, no calendars, no newspapers or change of seasons, it was sunny and mildly warm in the day, gently cool at night, he often missed his Blackberry and the internet.

One night after a seafood feast, they sat around playing gin rummy, he, Jed, Tom, Jane, Postman Dick, and Mia. Trent was bored.

"What's on the outside of town?" he asked.

"What?" said Tom.

"What's outside of town?" he said again.

"What do you mean, 'what's outside of town'?" Tom said again.

"I mean, what's outside of town, at the other end, beyond the woods," Trent said.

"Nothin that we know of," said Jed.

"There's got to be something, there's got to be another town or a warehouse where we get all our stuff or a power generator or something," he said.

"No one knows," Jane said and laid her cards down, "Gin," she said.

"You mean no one's explored it?" Trent said.

"No, why should they?" Tom said.

"To know what's out there, to find out who's running this town, where our supplies come from," he said.

"Is there something that you want?" Jane asked.

"I want answers, I want to know where I am, who's in charge, I'd like to go home," he said.

"This is your home, honey, we're your family now, whatever was before is gone, done with, and if there's anything you want, you just have to think about it for a few days and it'll usually show up," Jane said.

"Like the driving range, you wanted that," Jane said.

"Jane there wanted an old fashion saloon, Postman wanted a movie theatre and we got one," Tom said.

"Yea, you just have to ask," Jane said.

"Ask who?" Trent said.

They all sat silent.

"Just ask, out loud or think about it or talk about it like, 'hey, wouldn't it be nice if we had an ice cream parlor' and we will usually get one," Jane said.

"How about a bus out of here," Trent said.

Jane slapped him hard across the face, "That kind of talk we don't need here, you could mess it up for all of us," she said and left.

"You ask too many questions," Jed said and they all left him alone at the table.

Trent spent the next day at the driving range, hitting balls harder and farther than ever before. The range was at the end of town and the road wound into a thick of trees and disappeared. He heard no traffic, had not seen an airplane or even seen a jet stream. There were never any clouds in the sky. He stood at the edge of town, leaning on a putter and looked at the road, wondering what was beyond the trees. His stomach grumbled and he thought of the buffet and turned and went to dinner. He passed the new ice cream parlor that had opened up next to the café, the lights were dim but he could see the stools and soda fountains, large jars of candy lined one wall.

Everyone was already at the café, standing in line for meatloaf and cornbread. They all joked and laughed loudly, Jed finished early and began playing his banjo.

"How were your shots today?" Tom asked.

"I hit further than ever before, right on the money," Trent said.

"Congratulations," Tom said, stuffing his face.

"What are the chances of getting a good 18 hole course out here," he asked.

"I don't know, have you said anything about it?" Tom said.

"I've been thinking about it for a few days now," Trent said. "Do you think anyone else would play?"

"I don't think there are any other golfers here, it was never my game," Tom said, "but you keep thinking about it ok, it will probably happen."

The music slowed than went sour, they looked up and Jed was clutching his chest, he was pale and sweat poured from his body. Jane rushed over to him and eased Jed to the floor. Jed went limp and died. Jane laid his head gently on the ground and placed the banjo in the corner. Everyone stood and filed silently out of the café and went back to their room. Trent sat and stared at Jed's lifeless body for a few minutes before leaving.

The next day it rained. Dark clouds filled the sky and there was a steady, cold drizzle. There was a rack of large, black umbrellas by the door of the hotel and they each took one and walked down to the café, avoiding the muddy puddles that filled the street.

Jed was gone, his banjo sat as a homage in the corner. The chair had been put back at the table and the buffet was filled with fresh pastries, donuts, crepes and four kinds of gourmet coffee.

They tried to talk and joke but it was unspirited as they all sat and remembered Jed in silence.

"Where did he go?" Trent finally asked.

"Who knows," Tom said.

"Is there a cemetery around here?"

"Not that we know of?" Jane said.

"Maybe outside of town somewhere," Trent said.

"I said, we don't know and not gonna find out," Jane said and looked away.

"Hasn't anyone ever left here, hasn't anyone ever gone to see what's beyond the trees?" Trent asked.

"There was one feller who did, young guy like you, all full of questions and curiosity," Tom said.

"Yeah, he arrived one day, Dean or Daryl or something like that," Postman said.

"He was restless, we got a pool room with video games when he was here," Jane said.

"Yeah, but when he left, it closed down," Tom said.

"Where did this Daryl go?" Trent asked.

"No one knows, Postman there saw him walking out of town one day," Jane said.

"I called to him and he just kept walking, no one's seen him since."

"So, you don't know if made it?" Trent asked.

"Made it where?" Jane said.

"Made it…out of here?" Trent asked.

"Why would anyone want to make it out of here, we got all we want," Jane said.

"All you have to do is ask," said Tom.

Trent threw down his napkin and stood up, "I can't believe you people," he said and stormed off.

He rushed outside and stood on the sidewalk under the awning and watched the rain fall. The lights of the ice cream parlor suddenly lit up and circus music blared from unseen speakers. Trent walked back to his room, letting the rain pelt him on his head. He was soaked by the time he got to his hotel room, he lay on his bed all day long, listening to the rain.

The next morning he woke late, showered and went down to breakfast. The sky was overcast but the rain had ended. The café was full, but everyone sat quiet when he walked in.   Breakfast was a fruit tray and dry toast, the strawberries were wilted and the cantaloupe was dry. There was no butter or marmalade for the toast.

He got a cup of coffee that was thick and lukewarm. Everybody just looked up at him and nodded. They all finished their breakfast and left in silence, leaving him alone. Trent sat and nibbled on the toast and when everyone was gone stood and looked at the cold buffet. He picked up all the remaining toast and stuffed it in a grocery bag he'd brought, put some of the fruit into another and filled a whiskey bottle with water and headed out of town.

He walked past the saloon and the hotel, he saw their faces in the window and felt their eyes upon him. Elizabeth stood on the balcony of Room 4 and watched him pass. He got to the town sign that said Laramie. He turned and looked at the clap board town with its ice cream parlor, craft shop and music store. He saw the light fading, the music slowing,

The road ahead was dark. He glanced back once toward Laramie, heard the laughter from the saloon, and then treaded down the dark road that disappeared beyond the trees.

IX
▼

THE FINGER

"Get outta the way you dumb ass!" Kreg shouted as the black pick-up truck cut in front of him. He mashed on the horn and let it drone. Reaching out the window he shot the truck "The Finger," loud and proud. The truck driver slammed on his brakes and Kreg screeched his tires, trying not to smash into the ass end. Kreg jerked the Camaro into the right lane and sped past the truck, flipping the driver off again while mouthing "FUCK YOU!" He swerved around the truck and cut back into the lane just inches from the truck's front bumper.

"YEEE HAAA!" shouted Phil from the passenger seat.

Kreg looked in his rearview mirror and saw a big hairy arm flop out the window with the middle finger extended upwards, lazily. There was no style, no intensity, Kreg could tell he wasn't gonna do nothin'.

Kreg preferred the sharp knuckle "Bird," with the fingers pressed tightly against the palm and the middle finger towering over the hand, loud and defiant, shouting "FUCK YOU"! in capital letters. Phil's "Bird" was more like a fist with the middle finger extended and presented in an upward swooping motion. Everybody had a "Bird," but each one was a bit different in delivery and intensity, but they all said the same thing.

"Did you see that? That redneck just gave you the Bird man," said Phil and leaned out the passenger window and gave the truck two "Birds."

Kreg stepped on the gas and they sped away.

"OOOO EEEE! Did you see that, we showed that fucker didn't we?" Phil shouted.

"Hell, yeah."

"Oh, yeah. Two birds, out the window, in the traffic, at sixty miles an hour," Phil shouted over the radio, his adrenaline was pumping, the songs of Lynyrd Skynyrd blaring through the speakers. "My two birds trumped his fat, lazy bird."

"Free this bird, Redneck," Kreg said and sped on.

"I'm ready for some pool and some brew," said Phil.

They sped down the road to Benny's Pool hall, a red, neon rimmed concrete building with two small windows covered with burglar bars on the front. Kreg and Phil entered, each carrying a custom pool stick in a hard case. The place was dark and they stopped to let their eyes adjust to the sudden lack of light.

Slowly the familiar shapes of pool tables and the bar appeared, and they inhaled the smell of stale beer and sweat. The room was crammed wall to wall with pool tables, each one lit by a four-foot beer light covered with bottles and babes. On weekend nights, the tables were crowded with people shooting pool and hustling onc another. Everybody had a game.

A lot of money changed hands here, always under the table, gambling wasn't allowed but wasn't enforced either. Kreg and Phil did a lot of commerce in Benny's Pool Hall. Benny didn't care, just don't make it obvious. The only other rule Benny had was no fighting inside his place. Fighting was bad for business and hard on the tables. If you had to fight, you took it outside and quick, or Benny would take you outside and deal with it himself. Benny broke bones and enjoyed it. No fighting inside and no blood in his parking lot. Other than that, there were no rules, not for the pimps, the players, the girls or the dealers, just don't make it obvious.

Phil and Kreg went to the bar. Benny lumbered up to them. He waddled sideways like a crab, facing the bar so he could fit between the bar and the back-booze shelves. His massive frame scraped the sides more and more each year.

"Pitcher," Kreg said. Benny stopped to pour. There was only one kind of beer at Benny's. No one was sure what kind it was, no one ever asked. The last guy who ordered an import beer found himself on his back in the parking lot before he could say Heineken. But the beer was cold and cheap and after the first glass, it all tasted the same. Benny sat the pitcher and two frosted mugs on the bar and walked away to pour another pitcher for somebody else.

It was pretty busy for a nooner on a weekday; half a dozen tables had players at them. Kreg scanned the room. There were a few regulars, some guys from the Water Department hiding out until quitting time, some young guns, probably students from the college, a couple of dykes and an older guy that looked like Charles Bronson in his later years.

They chose a table in the back corner near the restroom, table number twelve. Kreg racked the balls while Phil gulped his beer and poured another one.

"You wanna break?" Kreg asked.

"Nah, go ahead." Phil said.

Kreg broke, sunk the fourteen-ball and started pursuing stripes. After sinking two more balls, he missed.

"Your turn," Kreg said. Phil was looking around the bar, watching the other games.

"What?"

"It's your turn."

"Oh." Phil stood, surveyed the table, looking for a shot. He tried to sink the two-ball in the left side pocket, missed, sat down and returned to drinking.

Kreg sank the ten and fourteen-ball but missed the thirteen and leaned against the back wall, waiting for Phil. Phil was still scanning the room and not paying any attention to the game.

"Your shot."

Phil stood, missed, sat back on his bar stool and poured another beer. Kreg missed an easy sixteen-ball.

"Damn. Your shot," Kreg said.

"I can see it's my shot. Don't you think I know when it's my shot? I don't need you remindin' me it's my shot. I thought we're supposed to be having fun, why are you riding me? Your shot. Your shot."

"Well, then, take your damn shot," said Kreg.

"Ok, ok." Phil said and hit the queue with too much force, scattering the balls before falling into the right corner pocket.

"You scratched," Kreg said.

Phil gave him a dirty look and sat down. Two guys wearing jeans and cowboy hats took the table next to them and started playing eight ball. Phil watched them intently. One cowboy wore a blue denim shirt, the other had a black shirt with colorful thread work swirling around the pockets. He was pretty good. The cowboy in blue couldn't hit nothing.

"Your turn," Kreg said.

"Ok," Phil said. "I think we could take these guys, you know, for a little cash. They're good, just not as good as they think.

"Nah, I just want to play a few games and get out of here," Kreg said.

Phil walked around the table, looking for a shot, spotted the two-ball near the left corner and walked around opposite. He studied the table and saw Kreg had sunk most of the stripes. Phil decided to try and run the table and began sinking the solid balls until he evened the count, two stripes, two solids and Mr. Eight-ball. Phil leaned over the table, intent on sinking the one-ball. The cowboy brushed up behind him, knocking his stick and spoiling the shot. The queue went wide left, missing the one-ball and stopping his run.

"Hey, watch it!" Phil said.

"Sorry, partner, I didn't mean to bump you," said the cowboy in blue.

"Sorry! Sorry! You made me miss a shot and my friend there don't allow re-dos. We had ten dollars on this game, and I think you ought to pay the man, since you just made me lose," Phil said.

"I said I was sorry, that's it, friend," the cowboy said.

"Friend. Friend? I ain't your friend," Phil said.

"Fuck you," said the cowboy.

"Naw, fuck you!" Phil shouted and stepped into the guy. Kreg reached up and pulled Phil back. "Come on, man, settle down, he didn't mean it. I'll let you have a redo, come on, just calm down and play some pool," Kreg said.

"Yeah, well, I ain't takin' no shit off some redneck faggot!" Phil hollered and the cowboy lunged at him. Benny appeared and grabbed the cowboy by the shirt and pulled him back. The cowboy turned, drew back his fist, looked at Benny and decided against it.

"Take this shit outside!" Benny shouted, looking directly at Phil.

"Up yours," Phil said to Benny.

"Yeah, up yours, now get out of here," Benny said, standing between Phil and the cowboy. Phil packed his stick and chugged his beer. Kreg gently pushed Phil towards the door, "Come on, let's go," he said.

Phil looked at him and smiled, then leaned over and shot Benny "The Bird." There was a sudden flash and a puff of smoke and Benny looked like a fat, burned up cartoon cat. His clothes were singed and smoking, his hair was fried and a little puff of putrid smoke rose from Benny's head. Benny looked at himself in the mirror, his skin was flash fried, pink and charcoaled.

"What the hell?" Benny said and looked up at Phil.

"What is this?" Kreg said, looking at his magic hands.

"Damn," Phil said with a laugh. Benny lunged at him and Phil ran towards the exit. The denim cowboy grabbed Kreg and pushed him into the wall.

"Hey, ass hole, I didn't do nothing," Kreg said and the cowboy came at him, fists clinched. Kreg grabbed the eight ball and threw it at the cowboy. The ball hit him in the forehead and he fell backwards.

"Fuck you!" Kreg shouted and ran towards the door. He turned and gave the cowboys a double bird, two middle fingers flying defiantly in the air. Kreg heard a loud POP and felt a rush of heated air. In a flash the two cowboys were charcoaled and smoking. Their clothes were burned and tattered. Their hats were gone and their hair was burned away, smoke rising from their scalp. They reached up and touched their singed heads. Kreg ran out of the bar, grabbing Phil as he passed. Phil was staring in disbelief and laughing.

"Come on!" Kreg shouted and jumped in his car. "What the hell was that?" He turned the ignition and they raced off, Phil was still laughing.

"I don't know, that was something though, wasn't it?" Phil said, examining his hands. "They pissed me off and I shot him the bird, and POOF! They went up in flames. It was all my anger suddenly channeled through my hands."

"I know, I gave them two cowboys the bird and they burned up," Kreg said.

"You know, I was watching Discovery Channel the other night, and they had a bunch of Faith Healers fixing people, channeling the Lord's power through their hands, maybe this is like that, though we're channeling…you know, something else," Phil said, starring at his hands.

They raced down the street and screeched to a stop at a stop light. "I can't believe this shit, man. Can you?" Phil said, still examining his hands.

They drove past an intersection, crowded with people waiting at the crosswalk. Phil spotted a ragged looking guy holding a sign that said, "Need mony, pleze Help." Phil shot him "The Bird" and in a POOF, like a lightning bolt, the beggar stood on the corner, charred and naked. His hair and clothes burned away in a flash. Phil could see the whites of his eyes as he blinked in disbelief, his face covered in black soot. Phil laughed at the blackened bum holding a burned up cardboard sign.

"Oh man, this is great!" Phil said. He leaned out the window and shot "The Bird" at people walking down the side walk, like a gun slinger with blazing six shooters. Each person suddenly flashed and turned into a charcoaled stick, alive, but dazed and singed all over, smoke rising from their charred body. 'Medium-well' thought Phil.

Phil sat back, laughing and exhilarated. He was examining his hands like they were brand new pistols.

A motorcycle roared up beside them and stopped. They looked over at the fat biker on his Harley. He wore leather chaps on his legs despite the heat, and a leather vest over a white, sleeveless t-shirt. He had long gray hair and a long, gray biker beard that covered his face. He turned and starred at them. Phil grinned and shot the biker "The Bird." Nothing happened. Phil tried again and nothing happened. The biker reached out and extended his middle finger at Phil. Suddenly, there was a loud WOOSH and Phil was charcoaled. His hair and clothes suddenly burned away.

"Ouch!" Phil shouted. "Damn, that hurts!"

"What happened?" Kreg asked.

"The biker shot me the bird and I got flamed, same as what happened to them cowboys," Phil said, looking at his smoking clothes and seared skin.

"Does it hurt?" Kreg asked.

"Hell yeah, it hurts. I just got flamed, man."

"You stink," said Kreg.

"Fuck you, my clothes and hair got singed."

"No, man your hair is gone," Kreg said.

Phil reached up and felt the stubble on top of his head. Just then they felt the car jerk. The biker stood beside the car, kicking the door with his heavy riding boots. They felt the car rock and heard the metal crunch.

"Hey, he's kickin' my car," Kreg said. The biker grinned and Kreg shot him "The Finger," and there was a loud POP as the biker exploded. His beard and hair was gone. His clothes caught fire and he began running and screaming.

"My eyes! I can't see! My eyes!" the biker. Kreg stepped on the gas and sped away, watching the big biker run around, as flames engulfed him.

Kreg sped away. "I can't believe this, what is happening," Kreg said. He slammed on his brakes as a red car cut in front of him, nearly hitting the front of his truck. Instinctively, he shot "The Bird," at the car in anger. The little red car suddenly exploded, as if hit by a bomb and it flew across the sidewalk. Kreg jerked the steering wheel to the right to avoid being hit. The car beside him honked and Kreg shot them "The Bird," as he passed, it too exploded into a fireball.

Kreg darted in and out of cars, scared and confused. He swerved too close to a blue Cadillac on his right. The driver swerved away and honked at Kreg and then shot him "The Finger," a loose fist with the middle finger extended. Kreg heard a rush of wind and a flash of pain and the sudden smell of acrid smoke. He looked down and his clothes were burnt and black. He looked at himself in the mirror and his face was covered in soot.

"Look what happened to me!" he shouted. "Look at this!" Kreg shouted.

Phil looked over at him with a laugh. "Hurts, don't it?"

Kreg stepped on the gas and sped towards the Caddie. He pressed on the horn and prepared to give the driver of the blue Caddie "The Bird." He clenched his hand into a tight, angry fist. He felt the thrill rise up in his stomach. He extended the palm into a Bruce Lee knuckle punch and felt an odd tremor in his body. As he began to extend his middle finger upward, he felt the hate and anger flow through him, felt the power course through his body and towards his hands. His thumb and fingers twitched against his palm as the middle finger rose into a half flight and pain shot through his body. A hot-flash overtook him, he could smell smoke and he quickly relaxed, eased off the gas and pulled in behind the blue car and let it speed away. He paused and let off the horn, his hand relaxed in mid-bird and the heat dissipated quickly.

"What was that?" Phil asked.

"I don't know. It was weird," Kreg said and pulled off the road and stopped. He got out of the car and leaned against a guard rail. He knew, somehow, that had he shot the man the "Bird" in all his anger, the Cadillac would have exploded, killing everyone inside and he too would have burned up. He'd felt the heat building, felt the pain. Phil got out and sat beside him.

A car passed by and honked and then tossed a beer bottle at them. It bounced off the car's roof just missing Phil's head.

"Hey, you Mother…" Kreg realized that Phil was shouting long strings of obscenities at the driver as his anger built. Kreg looked at his friend and saw the tight line of Phil's jaw, the flaring nostrils.

Kreg knew what came next and he shouted "NO!" just as Phil shot two "Birds" at the driver defiantly. They watched as the car explode and flipped end over end in a ball of flames. Kreg heard a shout and turned to see his friend suddenly explode, as if in slow motion, as rage and flames engulfed him.

Phil's screams got louder and then stopped. There was nothing left but the shadow of his friend as tiny ashes hung suspended in the air before falling into a neat pile on the ground. Cars rushed by and Kreg swayed in the rush of passing cars and he watched the wind slowly lift the ashes of his friend into the wind and blow him down the highway. Soon Phil was gone.

People in cars continued to rush by. A Suburban sped past and honked. Kreg flinched and instinctively started to shoot it "The Bird" and he stopped himself quickly and simply waved at the passing car. "Have a nice day," he said. "Have a nice day."

TORRID'S Gag Shop

Scrapbooking supplies for the discriminating scrap booker

- Tattoo frames
- Cutlery from the Ed Gein Collection
- Canopic Jars
- Hospital Replica Collection
- Canopic Cookie Jar Collection
- Sallykova Clamps

- Classic Collection
  Anubis
  Hapi
  Duamutef

Letters of authentication

Torrid's Gag Shop-San Francisco, Darfur, Bosnia, Moscow

X

▼

THE SLUSH PILE

The Long and Horrible Night

Book Review

By Chase Sanders

"Long Night on Horror Lake" the new book by Stuart Barfe' (pronounced Bar-Fay) is well…HORROR-BLE! It is long and horrible, boring and horrible, horrible, horrible, horrible. It has everything you would expect from Mr. Barfe', sex, romance, blood and gore (YUK), hairy monsters, dead things, slimy scenes and things that go bump in the night, everything but horror. There is nothing, repeat, NOTHING scary about this book. The characters are vain, shallow and stick like; the setting overly familiar; the plot predictable; the villain pathetic, sad and not scary.

Mr. Barfe' has produced three other titles in the nearly dead genre of horror fiction, each one making a brief blip on the Best Seller list before sinking back into the muck where it belongs. There is enough ugliness in the world; it does not need hack-writers, directors, artists or anyone else conjuring up new ways for the human race to be cruel to one another. We seem to be able to figure that out on our own. The mentally challenged trailer trash that finds thrills in the abomination of literature called 'horror fiction' can get their dose of ugliness from any daily paper, (this is on the assumption that they can read words with more than two syllables).

Faithful followers of this column know that I never review genre fiction, just as I never review pornography nor do I read tabloid newspapers in the checkout line. These are not the pastimes of the civilized or educated class. We should all contribute to the world and leave it better than we found it. With Mr. Barfe's previous success and his legion of fans, I felt I should give the genre and Mr. Barfe' an opportunity to impress. It was a mistake, a waste of time for this busy literary critic. This book contributes nothing to society, nothing to the world of literature and nothing new to the horror genre. Does this mark the end of his short career? I certainly hope so…

Chase Sanders rushed from the bus stop through the crowded downtown streets to his job at Crater Publishing. He carried his overcoat and umbrella in his hand as he hurried through the foyer. The morning influx of suits had passed two hours before. Now the lobby was crowded with people in search of their a.m. donut and latte.

"Hello Mr. Sanders, how about them Nix last night," said the guard from behind the counter.

"Worked late last night Gus, didn't get a chance to catch them," Chase said, hurrying towards the elevator.

"Oh yeah, Actress or Heiress, Mr. Sanders?" Gus asked.

"Actress," Chase said, grinning.

He glanced at his watch again, it was nearly 9 a.m. The editorial meeting began promptly at 9 o'clock, he would be at least 10 minutes late by the time the elevator took him to the 42nd floor.

The elevator was filled with office workers carrying $7.00 espresso and bagels to their offices. The elevator stopped on every floor, two people off, two people on, up one floor, three people off, two people on, up one floor. He would be at least 15 minutes late at this pace. Chase Sanders was tall and slender and was a foot taller than the other dark suited worker-bees. Like the others he wore black, a black suit, black shoes, a white shirt and thin black tie. The suit was cheap, but he wore it well.

The elevator finally stopped on 42, Crater Publishing. He rushed off. Rhonda, the red headed receptionist sat filing her nails. "They called for you 10 minutes ago."

"Thanks Love," he said as he walked past, she glared at him over her emery board.

He rushed to his office and flipped on the light switch. The room remained dark, they still hadn't replaced the fluorescent tubes. The tiny office had no windows, no pictures, no plants. Nothing but a small desk stacked with manuscripts and a lamp. Chase fumbled with the switch and turned the lamp on, it cast a small, dull circle of light across his desk and long shadows into the corner. Inside the office, to the left of the door were two metal drawers filled with reader reports, evaluations of books he had read. To the right of the door, standing nearly 8 foot high, was the Slush Pile.

The Slush Pile was the destination of unsolicited books, the hundreds of books submitted to the publishing company everyday by little old ladies, housewives, students, dreamers and would-be writers from all over the country. People without agents, people without contracts, people without talent. Books addressed to "The Editor," or the wrong editor or to dead editors ended up in his office, Chase Sanders with the inflated title of "Editor in Chief of New Talent Acquisitions."

The Slush Pile. No one wanted them, the books, no one asked for them, but they showed up every day by the cartful. Who knew, there could be the next Grisham or Joyce or Patterson in the piles, someone had to read them, someone had to try and find those diamonds in the rough, brush them off, shape them and turn them into best sellers. Chase was at the bottom of the editorial food chain and it was his job to review each and every one of them, to find that potential, publishing gold.

Chase stared at the pile of books. It was ten foot around at the base and nearly reached the ceiling. Piles of tan, brown and white envelopes sat waiting for him. Each day they brought more, each day some no talent housewife in the heartland added one more book to the pile. He glared at his demanding mistress. He grabbed one of the manuscripts from his desk and flung it at the pile in disgust. It bounced off the center and four manuscripts slid down like an avalanche. He grabbed his notes and ran off to his meeting.

The editorial meeting droned on for hours. He had nothing to report. He had not uncovered any best sellers, no Koontz's, no Clancy's, no Harry Potters. Each day he read through pages of dribble, each day he got a little older sitting in his little office reading books that no one wanted.

Chase grabbed a manuscript off the floor and sat at his desk. The red message light on his phone blinked. He touched the message button and opened the tan envelope and pulled the book out. The title of this little masterpiece was "Saturn Horse Café-A book of short stories." He turned the book over and pulled two pages from the back of the book for note paper and tossed the rest of the manuscript into the trash.

BEEP. "Hey Chase, Phil, we need to meet at lunch to discuss the PR trip for Dr. Evans. Call me..." He wrote the number on the back of the scrap manuscript pages and doodled while he listened to the remaining messages.

BEEP. "Hello... Mr. Sanders..."the voice was shaky, scared, "this is Jon, Jonathon Lepsky...I submitted my book of dog stories to you last week...I was wonderin' if you were gonna publish it..." Sanders hit the delete button.

BEEP. "This is Elliot Jackson," this voice was more confident, certain, "I sent you my novel about a prison basketball team, it's based on my real life adventures. I sent it to you over a month ago, and if I don't hear from you by the end of the week, I'm going to submit it to another publisher! Okay, Asshole, call me." Delete.

BEEP. "Mr. Editor...sir..." the female voice was frail and elderly, "I sent you a wonderful book on Russian cooking, who knew there were so many recipes for gruel. These recipes were passed down to me from my great-great grandmother and with each recipe is a funny little story about my family. I know there are a lot of people who would love these..." Delete.

BEEP. "Mister Sanders….this is Richard Starks..." the whiny voice was already under his skin, "Have you read my book yet? It's an epic novel of over 1000 pages about the drug culture in the 60's. If you like the book, I can change it up, I know it will make us a lot of money. Oh, I'll be starting a new book in a week or two. I just want to be a paperback writer and would appreciate..." Delete.

Damn writers, a bunch of whiney losers. They were cowards. Most of them holed up in back bedrooms and closets and wrote about a life they didn't live. Many didn't even have jobs. They depended on wives, parents or handouts from endowments or grants to fund their mental masturbations. They sat in their underwear and sucked on the Welfare teat of others while working on their "Great American Novel." There hasn't been a great American Novel written since Hemingway died.

The publisher took the risks, shelled out the money, booked the publicity. It was great editors like Chase Sanders that took a writer's emotional baggage and edited, rewrote, packaged and marketed the product to the masses. It was the editor who eliminated unnecessary characters and encouraged and improved other character and plot development. The author had no clue. He made books great, not writers. He could make anything a best seller, even some of the crap in the slush pile, but even his editorial powers had its limits.

He considered some of the titles on the New York Times Best Seller List, most of those guys couldn't pass a freshman creative writing class. They didn't know sentence structure, invented stupid plots and stick figure characters, but the public devoured it and bought their books en masse. He was the reason his writer's names were in newspapers and on talk shows and on the best seller list, John Paul Sanders not Whose-it Mr. Writer.

He hated sorting through the slush pile, but he had "discovered" several new writers and was anointed "King of the Slush Pile." A BA in English from Boston and a Masters in Literature from Columbia and he was stuck in Editorial Hell. Two years, he thought, he'd planned on two years paying dues, then on to working and developing his own stable of writers while making his own, unique contributions to literature and literary criticism. His unpublished novels were better than most of the crap on the New York Times Best Seller List.

Chase couldn't bear listening to anymore whining and begging or their sniffly little voices and deleted all remaining messages. He approached the pile with dread. The pile was taller than he was and got bigger every day.

Books submitted to the publishing house were first reviewed by readers, English majors hired fresh out of college, then if the readers enjoyed the book, they would send it up to the junior editors. If they liked the book, they would send it up to the associate editors then to the department editors, then to the title editors and then, finally to Mr. Crater's editors. If anyone along the way rejected the book, the manuscript was sent down a level to the editorial committee to debate its merits, hopefully find a champion and send it back up the editorial chain. This process took so long, many books were published posthumously.

Most books arrived through the basement, delivered daily by the ton by the US Post Office, Fed Ex, UPS or Granny Express. The large trucks backed up to the publishing docks and spit out the hopes and dreams of hundreds of aspiring writers from around the world. The A-list authors, the books people waited anxiously for, like King, Grisham, Rowling, Koontz, Leonard, Collins, Brown, and other best sellers came in the front door, carried in, often in secret to prevent theft or piracy, by highly paid agents, attorneys, or artist's representatives and occasionally by the author or the star themselves.

The bottom of the literary trough though was the unsolicited manuscript. Those dreadful first novels, the family histories of nobodies, the doctoral thesis' on the migratory patterns of the extinct Dodo bird and its impact on today's society, or anything addressed to "The Editor" ended up in the slush pile which resided in the corner of his office. It was his job to weed through the muck and return the hopeless ones back to their hopeless authors. Perfumed, coffee stained, dirty, nasty, smelly? Gone. Didn't like the person's last name, first name or city. Gone. Written by someone in a town that beat New York's hockey, baseball, football, or dart team, Gone. Flag waving religious freaks? Gone. San Francisco? Gone. Montana or Utah? Gone. He felt that any book addressed to "The Editor" should be returned. If the author didn't know the name of the editor who was over the product line they were writing for, they should not be published.

Once the manuscript made it past the envelope sort, those that were written in long hand, crayon, scribbled onto legal pads and stapled at the top were instantly returned. Those that were typed on notebook paper, were covered in Whiteout or had more than four misspelled words on the first page were also quickly returned. Colored paper, gone. Packed with stupid gifts like confetti, stuffed animals, gift certificates, gone, sans gift. Single spaced, gone. Small print, gone. Too heavy, too thick, too thin? Gone. Stupid cover letter? Gone. Begging? Gone. Any cover letter that started out, "this is my first novel, my wife says it is very good" gone.

There were three carts outside his door, three foot by five foot and four foot deep. They were marked "Trash", "Crap" and "Burn." The truly horrid submissions, manuscripts that were hand written, written with crayons or submissions that stole copy written characters or used tired, old plots were tossed into the "burn" pile and sent to the incinerator. Crap was returned to their sender with his personal stamp, "CRAP" in large red letters. He did this to discourage any more submissions from these particular writers. Some it deterred, some it did not.

The few books that made it to the "Trash" bin were simply returned to the authors, sometimes with a comment or two scribbled on the first page about how terrible their literary efforts were, but in Writerville, a personal comment from an editor, no matter how harsh, was like a gold star from the teacher, it acknowledged that a real live editor had actually read their work, had thought enough about it to personally comment on it and not simply stamped "CRAP" on it or sent a form letter. He didn't comment on too many books, it just encouraged the little worms to write more and resubmit, some thought his blistering comments were like invitations to the prom and established a relationship with a real editor and they called, sent post cards, made all kinds of offers to him if he would just publish their books.

On the rare occasion that he found a manuscript that grabbed his attention, he would take it home and read more than just the first two pages, fill out an Editorial Review form noting the merits of the book and outlining plot and characters. He would then submit it to the Editor.

He pulled an envelope off the floor addressed to "The Editor." He flung it into the Burn bin unread. Two more "To the Editor" were flung into the Trash bin. The next one was addressed to "Jim Sayles-Fiction Editor." He tossed it in the Burn bin. Jim was fired two years ago.

"Get yourself a new copy of the Writer's Market, moron," he said out loud.

The next manuscript was addressed in illegible cursive and landed in the "Crap" bin. The next envelope was neatly type and correctly addressed to him. It was from a "Mark Richey." He went to school with a kid named Richey, a big kid who used to beat him up at recess. He hated that kid. He flung the manuscript into the Trash bin. The next one was from Texas. He hated Texans and tossed it into the "Burn" bin. Anything from "The South" ended up in the smoke stack, "bunch of uneducated, gun toting red necks," he muttered under his breath. They couldn't write a proper query letter, how could they complete a decent book? "Here comes another 'prairie thriller' from Texas, yuk, yuk, yuk. Give it up hicks, the South lost and you can't ride your horses through town anymore.

The next book was addressed in a flowery cursive script with purple ink to the "Romance Editor" and smelled strongly of perfume. He tossed it into the "Burn" bin. The next book was from someone in Montana. He opened the book and used the pages to wipe the perfume smell from his hands, then tossed the book into the "Burn" bin. The next book was neatly addressed to him from a Jim Turner in Washington, DC. The name was familiar. He opened it. It was titled, "The Truth Behind the Lies of the Clinton Presidency by Jim Turner, former Personal Assistant to the Clintons, 1998-2001."

"Ah yes, I recognize the name now." He tossed it into the "Burn" bin. Not another Clinton-era diatribe. He was getting tired already and tossed the next ten books into the "Trash" bin without opening them. The next book was from Miami, Florida. The Miami Dolphins had beaten his beloved Giants this past weekend and he tossed it into the "Burn" bin.

The next book was written by a housewife in Oklahoma. The cover letter said her book was about her exploits as an extreme sex therapist, she was a devoted housewife and mother of two during the day and a wanton dominatrix at night and there was a picture of an attractive woman with long dark hair and skin tight leather pants and top. She was holding a long whip. The letter said her book was graphic and named names. Finally something interesting, he took a sip of coffee when the intercom beeped on his phone, it startled him and he spilled coffee across the top of the manuscript.

"Damn it," he said.

"Excuse me," the woman's voice said. Oh, no, he thought, it was Glenda, Mr. Crater's secretary.

"Ah, I'm sorry, I just spilled my coffee."

"Oh, Mr. Sanders, Mr. Crater would like to see you in his office."

"Ok, when?"

"Now," she said and buzzed off.

Great, he thought, he looked at the coffee slowly sinking into the housewife's manuscript and walked to the elevator, which seemed to take forever to open and rode it to the top floor.

"Good morning, Mr. Sanders," Glenda said, looking up from her computer screen. "Have you found the next Hemingway yet," she mocked.

"No, just a few Fitzgerald's and the next Patterson," he replied.

"Would you like some coffee?"

"Yes, two sugars and one cream," he said.

Glenda stood and strolled to the coffee pot, her split skirt dress more appropriate for a dinner date than a day at the office. She handed him a cup of hot coffee and he watched her as strolled back to her desk. He took a sip of coffee and nearly spewed it out. It was hot and black, no cream, no sugar. Glenda was smiling at him.

"Coffee ok?" she asked.

"Fine," he said.

The door to Mr. Crater's office opened and Nick, a junior editor ran out, his face red and his eyes wet as he rushed past them to the elevator. Mr. Crater looked around the room and said, "get in here Sanders."

Sanders walked into the office, his legs weak. Crater walked to his large, ultra modern desk that sat in the middle of the room, behind him, tinted windows from floor to ceiling looked out onto the world's biggest city below.

"Sit Sanders, this will take a minute." Sanders sat in a black leather chair that was low to the ground. Mr. Crater's towered over him, he could barely see over the top of the desk.

"Sanders, did you write a book review on Stuart Barfe's new book?" he said, picking up a thin newspaper from his desk.

"Ah, yes."

"And where did you publish this review?"

"I submit freelance work for papers all over the country, Mr. Crater."

"Yes, but where do you publish it?"

"Ah, not too many places," Sanders said, his face suddenly warm and flushed.

"And where all did you publish this particular book review?"

"Myrtle's Shopping News," he whispered.

"I'm sorry, I didn't hear you, where did you say?"

"Myrtle's Shopping News, in Garland, Texas."

"What exactly is the Shopping News?"

"It's a free weekly that publishes coupons and want ads and sometimes freelance articles."

"And where…in the Hell…is Garland…Texas?"

"It's, ah, near Dallas."

"And were you PAID for this review?"

"No sir, I'm still building my portfolio."

"Are you aware that Crater Publishing just signed Mr. Barfe' to a multimillion dollar, six book deal?"

"Ah, no sir."

"THE Stuart Barfe' who is the hottest selling horror writer since Stephen King?"

"Ah, no sir, I'm real…"

"SORRY? Are you SORRY that you just trashed the newest member of our literary A-List!"

"Yes"

"I am surprised that anyone even saw your little hatchet job, but somebody did and mailed it to Mr. Barfe'. Haven't you been warned about your little hobby?"

"I'm a serious literary critic…"

"Yeah right, I've seen your stuff. Look, no more writing, not book reviews, restaurant reviews, novels, short stories, poetry, Haiku, term papers or even shopping lists! I don't want to see your name in print anywhere. Do You Understand Me?"

"Yes sir."

"Your job is to manage the slush pile, to sort the unsolicited manuscripts by department and send them up to the editors. That is all."

"Yes sir, I've been doing that for several years now, I was hoping I could get moved into an Editor's position, maybe the fiction department."

Crater smiled at him and shook his head slowly back in forth in disbelief. "Sanders, do you remember that article that appeared in Time Magazine last year, the interview with J.K. Rowling?"

Sander's face got really hot and flushed. He felt his stomach drop and do somersaults. He remembered the article. No one ever let him forget it.

"Do you remember how she was talking about sending her unsolicited manuscript to over 12 publishers, and that someone from Crater Publishing, that someone I believe, after an investigation, was you, had written a note telling her how bad she was, how she should not quit her day job! How she should give up writing completely!"

"Yes."

"This nice, single woman who was raising her child on her own, working all day, trying to spend time with him in the evening, writing all night, and still just barely getting by. This wonderfully nice woman, I know, I met her once, tried to get her to come over to Crater Publishing for her second book. And do you know what she said? She didn't want to even talk to me after she found out which publishing house I was with. She didn't want anything to do with me or this company because someone had been so ugly to her. She said she almost quit writing because of the nastiness of the note. Did you know she still has the note? She keeps it framed in her writing den, she said it motivates her to try harder. Harry Potter has sold more books than all of Crater's publishing combined. COMBINED! Do you understand what a fuck up that is, that you are!?"

"I'm sorry Mr. Crater, I don't mean to…"

"Look Sanders, your dad and I go way back, and I've kept you on because I don't want him to know what a total failure you are, but one more screw up and you are out of here. Just sort the books, that's all, ok?"

"Yes, Mr. Crater."

"You owe me a Harry Potter. Go find it. Find me the next SOMEBODY! OK?"

Sanders took the long ride on the elevator, down to his little office, he got sideways glances from the editors on his floor, they all knew he had been "summoned," and it was never a good thing.

He entered the dark cave of his office. "Can I get a fricking light bulb for my office, please!" he said, his voice bounced off the bare walls and was swallowed by the slush pile.

The Diary of the Oklahoma dominatrix was soaked, the spilt coffee had penetrated all the pages and smeared the ink, it was an illegible stack of brown soaked goo. He put the picture of the housewife in his drawer and slid the manuscript into the trash can and dried the top off with a stack of paper towels. He dragged the remaining books into the trash can, deciding to start with a new stack.

He heard the voice down the hall.

"Special delivery for Chase Sanders, oh Mr. Sanders, special delivery from Steven King." It was Max, from the mailroom, the old geezer that kept the slush pile fed and piled high.

"Mr. Sanders," Max called out so everyone in the office could hear, "Steven King wants you to personally publish his next best seller." Max entered Chase's office and handed him the vanilla colored envelope:

TO: Editor-Best Sellers
From: Steven King
          2919 Portsmouth Ave.
          Maine…

"Very funny Max, this is Steven with a 'V' and not a Stephen with a 'ph' making this an anomaly. Max left, laughing hysterically. Chase hated his job. He stamped "CRAP" in red ink on the front and sent it to be returned without opening it, there was room for only one Stephen King, 'V' or 'PH' and this moron should have changed his name if he were going into publishing.

He stood beside the towering slush pile and extended his hands towards it like a roaring fire, (he could wish). He closed his eyes and tried to feel the vibes of a best seller, the flowing prose of a real wordsmith. He walked around the pile and hummed, trying to feel the call of the manuscript, tried to envision the color of the envelope, the style of text on the address label. Brown. Times New Roman.

Chase opened his eyes and in the dimness of the light picked ten, dark brown envelopes from the stack, each address printed in Times New Roman, he flung three dark brown envelopes with hand printed addresses into the "Burn" bin, wondering briefly if it could have contained a Nora Roberts or a Tom Clancy. He piled the ten, heavy envelopes on his desk, reached into his bottom drawer and poured a shot of Scotch into his coffee cup, even though it wasn't even noon. It had been a hard day already and would be a long one too.

The brown stack was a bust and all ended up in the "Burn" bin: three copyright infringed derivative compilations of Harry Potter, Harry Callahan and Harry and the Hendersons; one stole Dan Brown's famous detective and had him solving the mysteries of the Koran with Allah as an alien; two vampire novels; one cook book; one book was over 400, incoherent, hand written pages, in tight, neat script printed on front and back of each page. The first sentence read:

I HAVE SEEN THINGS YOU WOULD NOT BELIEVE,
THINGS IN BOOKS THAT SNARK FROM PEOPLE'S BRAINS,
A PASSAGE FROM THEIR DRAK WORLD INTO OURS HAS OPENED, BEWARE!!!!

Chase flung the book through the air and watched it bounce off the rim of the "Burn" bin stall right above the opening and fell into the heap giving Chase 2 more points, Chase 298, Writers zero. The next book was a western style novel set in the future, on Mars no less, that book landed in the "Trash" bin, giving the great Chase Sanders two more points his imaginary game of Book Baskets.

And the winner is…he held the last envelope, the last hope of the stack, the final brown envelope. He took a deep breath, willed this book to be "the one," and opened it slowly: "Personal Demons-A book of short stories by…" Christ on a Cross he said and flung the book across the room. Short stories. Short stories, nobody reads short stories anymore. Publishers don't want them; magazines pay the same as they did 50 years ago, .01 to .04 cents per word;

> Dear Mr. Short Story Writer,
>   Congratulations you're 3000 word story has won the literary lottery and been chosen out of the 5000 unsolicited, unasked for submissions this month and will be published next year sometime, maybe, and if we are still in business then, four months after publication, we will send you a check for a paltry fifty bucks, barely the price of a cheap blowjob in New York City.
> Congratulations looser!

Earth to writers, don't send me any more short stories, we don't care, we don't publish them unless you are famous and established and contractually we have to publish your short tomes to get your mammoth selling novels and people will buy anything with your name on the cover anyway. Don't do it. Don't. Resist the temptation. Take a deep breath, deeper and think about your idea. If your shallow little insignificant story can't sustain at least 190 pages, then make it a movie script, perseverance and IQ separates readers from the pop corn crowd. Short story writers are of the mindset that people with ten page attention spans can actually read with comprehension. No, no, no. They read People magazine and coupons, that's it.

He would have to write a brief summary of each book, author, title, page length, date postmarked, date read, topic and plot points, main character. He had been reprimanded for simply writing "Crap" in the summary section, although that summed it up pretty much, he thought.

Chase stood and stretched his legs. The office was quiet and he exited his dark, little cave and went to the snack bar. The office was empty, everyone had gone home, the lights were dim, it was past six o'clock. He walked to the soft drink machine in his stocking feet and put in a dollar, the machine hummed as it sucked the green bill in like a tongue, seemed to hiccup and cough and all the lights on the machine flashed and went dark. He pressed the button for a Diet Coke and nothing happened, pressed again, no response, he cursed it and pushed at it and cursed some more. No response.

He got a cup of water from the tap and returned to his office, halfway there he heard the machine hiccup and cough and then it seemed to hum at him. The darkness of his office was oppressive, he pulled two stacks of books from the pile and stood on them to reach the levers on the ceiling lights. He opened the panel and twisted the long fluorescent bulbs left and right, the bulbs hummed and flickered and with a quiet snap, went completely dark.

He reached up and closed the panel, flipped the last lever and felt the books shift, felt his balance change and began the slow tip-lean-fall and landed in the slush pile, several books tumbled down on his head. He flung those books into the "Burn" bin, two of them bounced off the wall and onto the floor. He stood and picked them up and flung them down the hall, watching the manuscripts twirl through the air in a slightly crescent curve. He liked the way they flew through the air and the sound they made as they crashed against the wall or the cubicle.

Pulling four more novels from the trash pile, he flung them like a Frisbee down the other hallway. He pulled a canary yellow envelope from the "Crap" pile, a hideous vampire romance sprinkled with bits of porn, he recalled from a 15 year old in Ohio. He flung it far, trying to have it curve around the large potted plant and into the hallway that lead to the conference room. It arched up by Boswell's office, seemed to hit an air pocket by Fran's office and increased its curve toward the conference hallway before losing speed and slammed into the planter. He cringed when he heard the crash. The next six manuscripts he tried to skip like rocks across the tile floor, but they just hit the ground and slid into the walls. A particularly horrible book, described by the author as a "Sci-Fi, historically accurate, romantic adventure," broke open and hundreds of pages went flying into the air. They floated like discarded feathers to the ground.

The hallway was a mess, typed pages littered the hall, torn, thick envelopes were scattered like stepping stones across the floor. He leaped from book to book in his stocking feet, sappy romance, predictable horror, inaccurate historical, teen lit, chic lit, witch lit, humorless humor, graphic crime novel and then he slid across a rambling fabricated political history like a skate board and landed at the Coke machine, it blinked at him, still holding his diet drink ransom. One more dollar and I'll give it up, it beckoned, one more dollar. He pulled a crisp green bill from his wallet, stuck it in the slot and the machine sucked it in like a snake withdrawing its long tongue. It hiccupped and coughed once and Chase pressed the button next to the Diet Coke, the machine flashed and went dead. "Damn machine," he said and returned to his office, he long kicked several manuscripts on his way back.

He decided on green this time and picked out the first ten green envelopes from the stack and started reading them. Another historical romance, a diary about the last days of the world set in post apocalyptic times, a book of short stories…

Outside the Coke machine hummed and belched out a soft drink. Chase heard it roll down the shoot and slam into the guard rail with enough force to make it spew for the next five minutes. In his office, a manuscript in a light brown envelope tumbled from the top of the pile and slid to the floor like a boulder rolling down a mountain, several books shifted from the impact and followed like a literary avalanche.

Chase returned to the next submission, a 250 page children's book. "Trash." The biography of some actor that made two appearances in two films, twenty years ago, "My Struggle to Stardom," it read. He'd wait for the sequel, "My Impossible Journey to Find a Publisher."

From the corner of his eye, in the shadows something moved, a shifting of envelopes in the pile, a subtle slide of a manuscript or two, he wasn't sure. The next book was a How-To book on Fishing (Strike 1) from a guy in Louisiana (Strike 2) with two first names (Strike 3) and he sailed the book into the "Burn" bin where it landed with a thump and then he heard, or thought he heard it flopping around in the bin like a stranded fish. The envelope slapped the others in a decisive manner, he got up and rushed to see and saw it flopping around the bottom of the bin and like a dying fish it jerked and flopped and slowly died. Behind him he heard a loud groan and he turned to stare into the animated face of the slush pile. Red manuscripts seemed to form a mouth across the base and others lined up to make a two eyes and a nose and it seemed to breathe and shift, the pile was alive.

The fish manuscript flopped around and Chase watched it and was suddenly struck in the head by a brown envelope-Dog Stories, Freda McCasland (42) Cincinnati, Ohio, 200 pages. Main story line concerns Bowser, the family's German Shepherd. He had the reader's summary in his head without even opening the envelope.

Chase was both amazed and confused by this when another one struck his left cheek. Italian Food, Pizza recipes from Grandma Denapolli, 236 pages, 50 recipes, written by Genoa Denapolli, her 26 year old granddaughter and dedicated to her grandmother. This book would sell he suddenly seemed to know, he could taste the pepperoni now but was struck on the back of the head by another book, nature book by a park ranger and the perils and triumphs he'd faced in the increasingly dangerous National Parks…another and another book flew at him and he absorbed, instantaneously the plot, main character, number of pages rushed into his skull, he knew the author's bio in detail as their life unfolded in his head, their hopes, their publishing dreams.

The slush pile monster let out a cry and the pile toppled down on top of him, covering him. He felt the weight of the words of all the manuscripts he touched rush instantly into his brain, he felt the pain and frustration of their efforts to tell their story and then the frustration they ran into as they tried to share that story, that ounce of wisdom and experience. His mood of wonderment changed to depression, deep and dark and scary as he entered the mind of the frustrated writer, the desperation of trying to complete their story, regardless of what it was, sports triumph or defeat, lovable dog stories, heroic historical, biographic, pornographic, the rush of stories struck him like a gavel and he felt hot, searing pain.

He tossed and kicked and tried to get the manuscripts off of his and the words tore into him like a tormented lashing. A large brown envelope latched onto his leg and began its path towards his throat, the manuscript burned his leg and the words crawled towards him like fanged spiders and each letter burned, each word was filled with hate and horror, and a grotesqueness reminiscent of Poe's demented mind. Those thoughts filled his, those words cut into him like Edgar's giant pendulum and as the manuscript got closer, the pain increased. A white envelope with brightly colored polka dots landed on his left arm and his mouth was filled with the sickly sweet taste of cotton candy and he felt something more horrible than the horror novel crawling up his legs. Clowns! The History of Clowns with over 250 photos, he screamed as he was bombarded with visions of rubber noses and flat hats.

He couldn't breathe, he felt trapped, his arms and legs immobile. He had a vision of being stuffed into a tiny car filled with clowns with big hair and large feet. He had to get out and fast, his mind was slipping and then something grabbed his leg and pulled. A thick, wet tongue snaked from the slush pile monster's mouth and pulled him towards the moving mandible made of manuscripts. Chase struggled and clawed at the ground to no avail. The creature pulled him into its giant mouth and everything went dark and the giant pile of unsolicited manuscripts fell down onto him. Chase absorbed the millions of words and heartache in those envelopes. In the instant before the slush pile crushed him, Chase knew what it was truly like to be a writer. The slush pile monster moved slowly back to its corner and let out a giant belch.

Two weeks after the disappearance of Chase Sanders, Lawrence Schlepnic showed up for his first day at work as the new Editor in Charge of New Fiction Acquisitions. He walked into the former office of Chase Sanders carrying a small box. He flipped on the light and nothing happened. The office remained dark. He set the box on the desk and flipped on the switch and felt the presence behind him. He jerked and turned around to stare into a pile of postal envelopes piled to the ceiling and 12 foot across. It sat there in the shadows like a waiting beast.

The slush pile sat in silence. He calmed himself and hung his BA from UT Tyler next to his MFA in creative writing from Boston U. He put the picture of his wife on the desk next to the phone and sat in the large, leather chair. He was a real editor, Lawrence celebrated quietly.

"Special Delivery for Mr. Schlepnic, Special Delivery for Lawrence S, ah Larry Schlep," Lawrence heard outside the door.

"Well hey, you the new guy?" the old guy asked.

"Yes, I'm Lawrence Schlepnic, the new Editor of Acquisitions."

"That's New Editor of *Unsolicited* Acquisitions," the man reminded.

"Ok, well what do you want?"

"Well hi, I'm Max and I have a special delivery from Bill Shakespeare."

"Oh yeah, really?" Lawrence asked.

"No, just kidding, get used to it kid, it can be brutal out here," he said and handed him a manuscript.

"What's that?" Lawrence asked, pointing to the pile.

"That, for you is job One."

"Huh?" Lawrence asked.

"That's the Slush Pile kiddo, the destination of unrequested dreams, but here there is no Santa Claus, no John Wayne, no last minute appeals," Max said. "You gotta start readin' 'em, evaluatin' 'em and sendin the good ones up the ladder, where maybe, in a long shot, one of these little jewels lights up and takes a name for itself."

"What happened to the last guy?" Schlepnic asked.

"No one knows, he just didn't show up one day, some think the slush pile got to him, everyday a little bit of unsolicited desperation crosses the transom and it can be bad. Find one or two best sellers in there and you're on your way. Pickin' books for a finicky public is the hardest jobs in publishing."

"Well, where should I start?" he asked.

Max grabbed the envelope closest to his left hand. "Start with this one," he said and handed him a crinkled, dark brown envelope addressed to "The Editor," in tight, cramped letters and left.

The envelope was from a C. Sanders, no return address. Lawrence opened it up and looked inside and pulled the manuscript gently out. It looked to be about 400 pages and he noticed that each page was handwritten in tight, block letters.

I HAVE SEEN THINGS

The cover letter said.

THINGS YOU WOULD NOT BELIEVE, SCENES FROM THE IMAGINATION STORIES DESPERATE TO BE HEARD HEAR MY STORY IF YOU DARE

XI

▼

TRIBES

From behind a bush, Preston shivered. He peered into a clearing, lingering in the shadows of the forest. He was attracted first by the fire and as he got closer, the smell of food. He crawled quietly from tree to tree. He heard the voices of men and he moved closer, trying to hear.

Three men sat around a fire pit. Flames darted like tongues into the air while their long shadows danced like ghosts on the surrounding trees. Preston smelled meat and coffee and his stomach grumbled. He had not eaten in two days. He crawled closer on his hands and knees, cutting his hand on a rock and stifled a groan.

"Across the creek...massacre...no survivors," he overheard the men say. "They were American and didn't seem afflicted." He watched as one, wearing a cowboy hat, cut meat from the spit. Another, a dark skinned man wearing a red flannel shirt and a baseball hat, turned the spit slowly and the juices fell into the flames and spat and hissed back at them. They drank their coffee and ate in silence. The third man, a skinny guy with long hair stood and poured more coffee into his cup and looked up into the clear, night sky.

Preston's mouth watered, he inched forward. He crawled across a branch that snapped beneath the weight of his knee, it cracked loudly in the night. The men around the fire did not look up. Preston saw they had tin cans sitting on rocks near the fire, beans and corn, potatoes perhaps. He clutched his stomach as it grumbled and cramped.

Above his head he heard another crack, but this was the unmistakable sound a rifle made as the hammer was cocked and ready to fire. He looked up into the dark barrel of the gun.

"Don't shoot me, please don't shoot me," Preston mumbled. "I don't have anything. I haven't eaten in days. I saw your fire and…"

"Shut up," said the man with the rifle, "move!" he said and motioned with the rifle for him to go down to the fire. Preston stood slowly, putting his hands into the air and walked into the clearing.

The men quit talking as Preston and his captor approached.

"Hey Mel, lookie what I got," the man with the rifle said. "I found him eyeballin' us from over yonder."

The man with the cowboy hat looked at him and asked, "Is he afflicted?"

"Nah, don't seem to be," said the man with the rifle.

"Bring him closer, Burt," Mel said.

"Lookie at em Mel, he's a fat one," Burt said, poking him with the rifle.

"Burt, be nice," Mel said.

"He sure 'id be a good un, huh? Well?" Burt said.

"Burt, he's a guest for the time being, bring him over here," Mel said.

Burt stuck the rifle in his back and gave Preston a little shove. Preston stumbled down the rocky incline and fell in front of the fire.

"What're you doing out there?" Mel asked.

"I saw your fire, I've been wandering around in the woods for two days. I'm lost," Preston said.

"Who you with?" Mel asked. Preston watched the man in the flannel shirt approach as he pulled a large hunting knife from a sheath he wore on his belt.

"Nobody. I'm alone, I swear," Preston said, his hands still up in the air.

"Well, where's your family?" Mel asked.

"They're dead, all dead, they died in the attack," Preston said.

"Then, why aren't you dead?" Mel asked.

"I was…I was in a meeting when it happened, away from the city. I was far away from the blast. My wife, Sarah and two daughters were in our apartment, downtown, they died in the first wave," Preston said.

"I'm sorry to hear that," Mel said. "My name's Mel. This here is Jose" he said, pointing to the man in the flannel shirt, "and that's Doc," he said, pointing to the tall, skinny man. "You already met Burt, there."

"Yes, ah, we, already met," Preston said.

"Come by the fire, have a seat. Are you hungry?" Matt asked.

"I haven't eaten in days…I haven't smelled cooked meat in…well, I mean I haven't smelled…" Preston said and broke into tears.

"Now, come on there partner, I know what you mean. We've all been through a lot. Jose, fix our guest a plate," Mel said.

Jose cut a large slice of meat from the spit and handed it to him on a tin plate. Jose was dark skinned and had dark hair and a young face. Preston grabbed the meat and began chewing greedily. He tore into with bare teeth and growled softly.

"Give our guest some of them beans, will ya' Jose and see if he'd like some potatoes, maybe a little coffee. Would you like some coffee?" Mel asked.

"Yes, it smells so good," said Preston.

Jose spooned hot vegetables onto his plate and poured coffee into a tin cup. Jose and Mel watched Preston devour his food. Burt sat by the fire and got a cup of coffee, but still kept the barrel of the gun pointing at Preston.

"What's your name?" Mel asked, after Preston had finished eating.

"My name's Preston, I really appreciate the food, and for not shooting me," Preston said.

"I'm glad we didn't have to," Mel said. "We've had to shoot a lot of afflicteds. Them sons-a-bitches are crazy, kill you just for the sake of killing."

"Kill ya' real messy, too," said Burt.

"I heard a bunch of people shouting and howling in the woods the other day," Preston said.

"When was that?" asked Mel.

"About three days ago, over near Pointer," Preston said.

"That's about ten miles south of here," said Mel.

"They broke into my lake house and trashed the place. They stole everything and set it on fire," Mel said. "They came busting in the front door and I ran out the back. I hid in the forest until they left."

"Good thing you did. They would have killed you just to hear you scream," Doc said. Doc moved nervously around the campfire. He leaned against a tree and listened for a minute and then began pacing again in jerky movements.

"Why? What's wrong with them?" Preston asked.

"They're afflicted, that's what. Are you some kind of idiot," Burt said.

"Something in the bombs," Mel said, "something more than radiation."

"I heard they were annihilating the cities, New York, Dallas, LA, Seattle, it was happening all over," Preston said.

"Yeah, in the cities, big concentrations of people who didn't die in the blast got exposed to the other agent. It made them crazy, turned them all into killers," Mel said. "We got some fall out, carried out here by the winds, but I think most zones are safe now, at least for exposure to the affliction."

"You still got bands of those crazies running around. We hadn't been able to kill them all," said Burt said.

"Where you from?" Mel asked, pouring more coffee into Preston's cup.

"New York, I'm from…was from New York," Preston said.

"What are you doing out here?" Doc asked.

"I have a house on Lake Athens," Preston said.

"I thought you were at a meeting," said Doc.

"Well, I was…I was in a…a meeting."

"At your lake house?" Doc asked, moving closer, his whole body seemed to twitch.

"Yeah, my secretary and I were doing some work…ah…away from the office."

"Preston, you old dog you," Mel said and slapped him on the knee.

"No, it wasn't' like that…"

"Sure it was, admit it, come on Preston," Mel chided. Jose sat by the fire and listened quietly.

"Ok, she was making overtime," Preston said with a sly smile, "we were spending the weekend at my cabin when the bombs went off."

"What do you do in New York to get a secretary?" Mel asked.

"I'm a C.O.O," Preston said.

"A C-O-O, what's that?" asked Doc.

"Chief Operating Officer. He usually runs the company while the CEO is going out to dinner on Wall Street and accepting awards" Mel said.

"Exactly," Preston said.

"What happened to your secretary?" Doc asked.

"She…she…well…we heard about the blasts on the radio, all the major cities."

"Yeah, the terrorists had it planned, one city after another, hour after hour, another news flash, another city gone," Mel said, staring into the fire.

"It was all over by the time we turned on the radio," said Preston. "The death of America in one afternoon."

"I wouldn't say America's dead," Mel said. "I'm American, I'm still here. You're American, you're still here, Jose there, well, Jose won't be needing any immigration papers anymore. We might need some to cross his borders…but…"

"Did the terrorist hit anywhere else?"

"No, just the U.S. from what we've gathered, but if they can wipe out twenty-five major U.S. cities in one day, it won't take them long to hit Britain, Japan, China, Israel. Any place they want," said Mel.

"Oh, my God," Preston said, his hands trembling so much he spilled hot coffee all over his hands. "Damn it!"

"So you lost your family in the blast?" asked Doc suddenly.

"Yeah, downtown high-rise apartment. Radio said there were ten blasts around New York City. Killed nearly everyone in the city."

"Your wife included?" Mel asked.

"I'd guess so, my apartment was only two blocks from one of the blasts," said Preston.

"You guess? What do you mean, you guess?" Doc asked, his body nearly spastic as he spoke.

"I mean, they were at the apartment, or shopping, or at a restaurant somewhere downtown when the blasts went off. They would have died instantly," said Preston.

"But you don't know for sure?" Doc asked.

"No, no I didn't go into the city, not after hearing about all the reports of radiation and gangs of crazy killers running loose," Preston said and took a deep gulp of java.

"What did you do?" Mel asked.

"My secretary, Kim…Kim and I, we just hid out, there was nothing we could do," Preston said.

"Where is Kim?" Doc asked.

"What?" Preston asked.

"Where's Kim? Your secretary," Doc asked again.

"She, well, she ran…she tried to run when the crazies came…she tried to run out the back but they caught her…" Preston said.

"They caught her?" Mel asked.

"Yeah, they caught her in the house."

"Where were you?" Doc asked.

"I…ah…I was in the woods…she didn't get out in time."

"But you did? How did that happen, Preston?" Doc asked, getting into his face.

"I got out first. Kim thought they might be friendly and went to the door. I told her not to open the door and went into the kitchen for a knife when they broke in. I couldn't do anything for her. I couldn't have saved her, they…they were vicious. I couldn't stand the screaming, so I ran out the back into the woods and wandered around for days, forging what I could, hiding when I had to. You've got to understand, there was nothing I could do."

"Nothing you could do for your secretary, nothing you could do for you wife and kids, you're not much good for nothin', are you?" Doc said, his body twitches got worse.

"Now, Doc, settle down. I'm sure Preston assessed the situation quickly and made his decision. You got to be able to think on your feet to be a…a C-O-O, don't you?" Mel asked.

"Yeah," Preston said quickly.

"I don't know if we really need a COO. What do you think?" Doc asked.

"What, what do you mean?" Preston asked. "You're not going to kick me out, are you?"

"Not exactly," Mel said.

"What do you mean by that," Preston asked.

"It means resources are scarce and we have to utilize everything we can to survive," explained Mel.

Preston looked at the men. He saw Burt coming out of the trees towards them. He looked at the meat on the spit. He realized it didn't look like deer or cow.

"Wait a minute, look, I'm worth a lot of money, I can get you some, all you want," Preston said.

"Really?" Doc asked. "We could use a few stacks of cash."

"Yeah, American greenbacks are real good for starting fires," Burt said.

"Starting fires? You're crazy," Preston said.

Jose walked slowly towards them and pulled his long knife from the sheath. His stares bore holes through Preston.

"Yeah, that's all it's good for, there is no economy now," Doc said.

"Yeah, it's a new, world, order," said Mel.

"Look, I'm an important person…"

"Yeah, that's what you keep saying," said Doc.

"A C-O-O, I think you said, of what?" asked Mel.

"I was the C.O.O of a manufacturing company. I'm worth a lot of money."

"How much?" Mel asked.

"Millions. I'm a millionaire, several times over," Preston said.

"What did you manufacture?" Mel asked.

"We manufactured tractors in Mexico; we had a gun factory in Poland; refrigerators in China; cars in Kuwait; electronics in Japan," Preston said.

"Wow, that's a lot of manufacturing," Mel said.

"Yeah. So?" Burt said.

"So, I've got an MBA and a law degree," said Preston.

"Well I got an H&K from England and an AK-47 from China," said Mel.

"And a PhD in BS," said Doc.

"You built cars, we got a truck we can't get to run, think you can fix it?" Mel asked.

"No, no, I didn't build them myself, I ran the company that did."

"Oh, so YOU didn't build the cars," Mel said, concerned.

"No, don't be silly, I don't know the difference between a monkey wrench and a crowbar," Preston said.

"Well, do you think you can fix guns, we got some guns need repairn'," Mel said.

"No, I never even went to the gun plant, I got it in a takeover bid and hadn't had time to sell it off yet."

"Oh, I see, well, what can you do, Preston?" Mel asked.

"What do you mean?" asked Preston.

Mel stood up quickly and grabbed the pistol from his holster. Jose came closer with a knife in his hand. Burt ran up with his rifle cocked.

"Hey, wait a minute," Preston said. "What seems to be the problem here?"

"The problem here is we can't take on excess baggage. We don't have the food or the resources, so I'm askin' you what you can do?" Mel said.

"What I can do?" Preston stuttered.

"Can you fish?" Burt asked.

"No."

"Can you hunt?" asked Mel.

"No."

"Well, you can't fix a car, repair a gun, you look too fat to be much good in a fight, or run from one if we was losin'. So I don't think you're good for nothing but shootin'."

"Wait a minute, wait a minute. Look, I ran a multimillion dollar company. I had thousands of employees from all over the world. I did budget, operations, planning, marketing."

"So, Doc there's a C-O-O too." Burt said.

Preston looked at the tall, nervous guy.

"Yeah, Doc there ran a multimillion dollar, worldwide, distribution operation, and he did it across borders, right underneath the noses of the Feds." Mel said.

"What?" Preston asked.

"Doc there had a drug manufacturing organization in Columbia and a distribution operation from Florida to LA. He brought in drugs from China and Afghanistan and other places," Mel said.

"Yeah, and he's a millionaire too and he don't pay no taxes," Burt said.

"Well, neither did I, it just takes a good tax attorney," Preston said.

Burt struck him in the face with the butt of his rifle and Preston fell down to the ground. "I'm tired of messin' with this guy, he just likes to talk, like that actor fellow we had here last week," Burt said angrily.

"Yeah, what was that guy's name, he was in all those action movies. What was his name?" Mel asked, snapping his fingers as if it would help him remember.

"Jim Kilado!" Mel said remembering.

"Yeah, that's it. He couldn't do none of it any ways, it was all stunt doubles and trick cameras. He was useless," Burt said.

"Where is he?" Mel asked, wiping the blood from his face.

"Oh, he's gone," Burt said and smiled.

"I can't believe you had a place on Lake Pointer and you don't fish," said Mel.

"Nah, I worked all the time, to pay for it all," Preston said.

"Didn't you ever take your kids huntin' and fishn' out there?" asked Burt.

"No, no time," said Preston.

"But you had time to take your secretary out there, huh?" Burt said. "I think we ought'ta shoot him now, get it done before Billy Joe and Ian get back." He aimed the gun at Preston's head.

"Now wait, wait a minute. I'm an executive, a C.O.O. of a major company. I got degrees from Harvard and Yale. That's got to count more than…than say that Mexican there, or that back woods bastard right there," Preston said, pointing to Burt and Jose. Jose just stared at him.

"Jose there snuck in to America after they built the fence and had border guards all over the place. Jose started out digging holes with a shovel and in less than a year was operating heavy machinery. He learned English, which makes him bilingual. How many languages can you speak?" Mel asked.

"Just English," Preston admitted.

"Besides that, he's a Hoss. He can work twelve hour days in the sun with a pint of water and no food. Lookin' at you, you're overweight, out of shape and I would bet a diabetic, which means you are on a special diet and medicine."

"Yeah," Preston said.

"Burt there can shoot running squirrels out of the trees in the dark. Then he can make it taste like steak. You can send him into the forest and tell you what green plants make good salads and which ones'll kill ya.

Doc there, well, Doc is very resourceful. He's a numbers whiz, knows what plants will make you drunk, which ones will make you high and he's pretty good with a knife."

"Yeah, well what do you do?" Preston asked.

"Me, I guess I'm the brains of the operation, sort of like the C.E.O. of this little posse," Mel said. "I can also repair tractors and cars. See, I used to work at that tractor factory, before you laid everyone off and moved the plant to Mexico. Then I opened my own gun shop, so I'm pretty resourceful, Preston, and I guess there's just no room at the top for two," Mel said and walked back to the fire, leaving him alone with Burt, Doc and Jose.

Joe Bob and Ian came out of the wood at dawn with their guns slung over their shoulders. They moved slowly and quietly, they were tired. Mel watched them come in and gave them a wave.

"Hi boys, how'd it go?" Mel asked.

"It was quiet, didn't see no Crazies walkin' around, just that one guy that Burt brought in, but he looked like he was handlin' it, so we just kept watch," Joe Bob said.

"Yeah, quiet night," Ian said, and yawned. "I'm starved," he said walking towards the pit.

Jose stood by the fire, turning the spit slowly, letting the juices fall and sizzle in the fire.

"What's that?" asked Ian

Mel looked at him and said, "That's Preston, he's the COO of the company I used to work for."

Ian's mouth began to water. "An executive, sweet."

XII

▼

FAME

The music played on in his head, the songs he'd written, the songs he'd sang to cheering crowds in cities all over the world. The music played on and on as he stared into the darkness and tried to forget his life. He tried so hard to drift off to sleep and yet that final rest eluded him and so he laid there and continued to stare into the dark.

Tiny flakes of satin fell onto his eyes like rain and slid across his face. He tried to ignore it but the edges of the faded material was rough and felt like insects crawling down his cheek. The ever present sound of the worms as they feasted on their moist buffet was all around.

"Hey Monty, you awake?"

Fremont never shut up. He talked day and night and never let up.

"Monty, Monty, tell me 'bout the Chicago concert again, 'bout the blonde. Monty, come on man, talk to me."

Monty ignored his neighbor and retreated into his memories, of blondes in Chicago, redheads in Cincinnati, recording in LA, all set to the tune of "Our Love Will Last Forever."

The night finally past and dawn was fast approaching. He could feel the cool dampness of the morning as the fog crept slowly over head. Fremont had given up his quest for gab and drifted into memories, the worms had ceased their wet whispers and had, no doubt made their way into the grass. He hoped they crawled into a swarm of hungry sparrows, the bastards.

His bones had been cleaned chalk white beneath his trademark black tuxedo.

The tuxedo itself had begun to deteriorate. Time moved slowly, infuriatingly slow, interned in a silver casket, six feet beneath the soil he lay, as if paralyzed, the soft jelly of his eyes devoured long ago by long crawly things.

"Hey Monty, you awake?" Fremont said in a hushed voice, as if others would hear, as if anyone in the grave was capable of sleep.

Monty didn't answer, hoping Fremont would leave him alone.

"Monty, do you know what day it is?" Fremont asked.

"No."

"I think it's moving day, I heard the diggers over on South Hill."

"I don't really care, Fremont."

"Fresh meat," Fremont said at full volume.

"Do you always have to say that? It's vulgar."

"Ah come on, Monty, we were all fresh meat once, newbies, new comers, the newly deceased."

"I would not wish that on anybody."

"Hey, dying's just a part of living, everyone does it."

"Yeah, but it's not what any of us expected."

"Not true Monty, if you read your scripture, it promised life after death."

"You're a sick Fuck, Fremont. This isn't living, it isn't dead, it's just…just dull."

"Yeah, but its Saturday, fresh meat day."

"I don't relish in another's pain as much as you."

"I just think it's funny, the transition, like all us deadsters are hiding in the closet and when the rookies reach awareness, we all shout, 'Surprise!'.

"And what does that accomplish? What?"

"Well, nothing, but we all went through it, had to make the adjustment, reconfigure our cosmic constitutionality and reach realization."

"It's more like a cosmic fucking. I'm tired of all this."

"You're such a bitter old fart, Mr. Hollywood, Mr. Face-in-Bright-Lights, Mr. Famous."

"That's what got me here."

"No, death got you here, fame has kept you here."

The ground began to rumble and shake and the noise of diesels blocked the chance of further conversation. The digger pounded at the hard, dry earth and cracked a hole in the surface, its long arm struck at the ground with its metal claw and tore a deep gash into the earth.

"Sounds like we're getting a neighbor," Fremont shouted.

The big Cat dug a four foot by eight foot hole in the ground that was exactly six feet deep in two sweeps of the giant claw and drove off. Monty and Fremont could hear the workers talking overhead.

"Hey Cuz, grab that tarp and cover up that dirt pile."

"What, why?"

"Cause that's what you get paid to do and we don't want the guests getting graveyard dirt all over their Sunday finest."

"Craig, man, I can't believe I let you talk me into this gig."

"I tole you, I tole you for you came."

"No, you didn't say nothing 'bout me diggin' no graves, this place gives me the creeps."

"Theys all dead."

"Yeah, that's the part that creeps me out."

"I ast you if you wanted to make some easy money…"

"Yea but you didn't say nothin' 'bout workin' in no grave yard. I swear I hear them whisperin', when it gets all quiet, just beneath the wind it sounds like them ghosts are talking to each other."

"Cuz, I tole you not to be hittin' the bottle 'fore noon. You start talkin' crazy."

"I ain't talkin' crazy, but this place is makin' me crazy. I'm gonna finish b-b-b-bury'n this one, then I'm out of here and don't you never ast me to help you no more."

"Come on Cuz, it ain't that bad, I been doin' this for years, somebody's gotta do it, people gonna be dying, same people gonna need bury'n. We might as well make some money."

"Money don't matter to me now, getting' home without seein' no ghosts what matters. What time's this service?"

"Three o'clock."

"Three o'clock! That means we might not get outta here till after five. I ain't gonna be caught in no graveyard after dark, no siree, not me."

"Oh come on Cuz, I been here plenty of times after dark, nothin' happin' here, they all dead."

"You ain't never heard nothing, never seen nothing here at night?"

"Nah, 'cept this one time."

"Naw, no way, you ain't be tellin' me 'bout this one time', there ain't gonna be 'this one time,' I'm outta here."

Monty heard his voice trailing off, heard his footsteps running south, towards the entrance of the cemetery.

"Son of a bitch," Monty heard Craig say as he tossed a few shovels of dirt out of the pit, making the sides clean and true.

Fremont suddenly let out a long, low moan; the sound rattled the metal on the casket. To Monty, the sound was deafening, but it would be barely audible to the mortals if they were sensitive. The shoveling stopped.

"Cuz, is that you? You come back?"

Fremont continued his parlor trick, long, low-frequency moans.

"Cuz, come on Cuz, cut it out, I'm not foolin'" Monty heard him say and then the patter of his feet as he bolted towards the entrance.

Fremont's moan turned into wild, snorting laughter.

"Would you shut up," Monty said.

"Oh, ha, I love that one, I think the low frequency moans have the most impact, it's hard for them to hear the higher pitches, but the low ones sneak up on them, and they realize it's not just the wind. That's the trick, low moans, took me years to figure it out, then, when their listening, you can pop a few banshee screams on their ass and that's when they freak out"

Fremont's laughter faded with the day and was drowned out by the low rumble of cars, like a motorized caterpillar crawling slowly through the headstones. The cars stopped on the lane and Monty heard the slam of car doors and the light patter of footsteps overhead. Family and friends of the deceased gathered overhead and the mutter of solemn words were passed and then the patter of footsteps leaving, the slam of car doors and the caterpillar of cars crawling down the hill and then they were gone. So sad, Amen, good bye.

"New guy didn't have many friends, did he? That's sad, man, sad. Hey did you hear those lame-o words that preacher said. 'Ah didn't know the deceased vary well, he wasn't' much on church, but that don't make him an evil man, or a Godless man.'"

"Amen," the mourners said.

"But ah'm told he was an honest man, a good man, a Gawd fearin' man. May da boy, rest in peace, A'man.'

"No, my hearings not so good anymore, I'm starting to fade a bit I think," Monty said.

"Naw, not you, the illustrious Monty Compton, crooner to kings and hotties all over the world, you'll never be dead man, you're famous, you're gonna be here a long, long time."

"I hope not."

"I'm sorry our little party here is not good enough for the great Monty Compton. You're probably used to much finer company than us grave rats."

"You know, I don't miss all the parties, the booze, the drugs,"

"You're killin' me man."

"Really, it was great for a while, a real short while, but then it got old."

"Oh yeah, right. Partyin' with the most beautiful women in the world at some of the most famous spots on the planet and you're bitchin.' Hey Evan, can you believe this guy." Evan lay two graves over from Fremont.

"You boinked Mellissa Madson didn't you," Evan asked.

"Did he just say boinked? Monty, did he really say boinked?" Fremont asked.

"I didn't 'boink' anyone," said Monty.

"He didn't 'boink' anyone, but he fucked half of California. Hey, Monty, is it true you had a thing with Rock Hudson?" Fremont prodded.

"Monty and Rock?" Evan parroted.

"Shut up. I wish you guys were dead."

"We are!" Evan and Fremont said together.

"Shut up, I wish I was dead," Monty said.

"You are!" they said together laughing.

"I mean really dead, not this," Monty said.

" A H H H H H H H H H H H H H H H H H H H H H H H H !
AHHHHHHHHHHHHHHHHHH !

"New guy's awake," Fremont said.

"HEEEEELLLP! HEEEEELLLPP! I can't move, I can't see, HELLP, HELLP."

Fremont started laughing his ass off.

"Would you shut up, you remember what it's like," Monty said.

"Yeah, Fremont, it's like waking from a bad dream into a nightmare. Cut the new guy some slack," Evan said.

"Hell no, remember Walter?" Fremont said.

"Yeah, old fart two stones over." Evan said.

"He gave me Hell. He was the only one on this side then, so there was no one else to talk to, son-of-a-bitch. After I awoke, I'm layin' there in the dark, can't move my legs, can't move my arms, can't scratch my face, can't turn my head or blink or open my mouth and I hear this low moan, low and lonely like and I can't figure out where it was coming from. It's like everywhere, all around me this low moaning, like ghosts in the ground."

"Yeah, ole Walter could scare the be-Jesus out of me, he had the best low moans of anybody," said Evan.

"He kept that up for days, non-stop and then I discovered I could scream, my mouth was stitched shut but I found I could scream, like I learned I could see with my eyes glued shut."

"Like you're dead, but not really, like your alive, but more dead. Weird man," Evan added.

"AHHHHHHHHHHHHHH! AHHHHHHHHHHHHHHHHHHHHHH HHHHHHHHHHH!"

"Just like birth, but with awareness," Evan said.

"WOOOAH! WOOOOOOOOOAH!" Fremont started his low frequency moans that shook the ground. The screams from the new guy ceased.

"What? Huh? Who's there?"

"WOOOOOOAH!" Fremont continued.

"Would you cut it out?" Monty said.

"SHHHH. WOOOOOOOOAH!"

"Help! Someone. Help!" he shouted.

"WOOOOAH!" Fremont moaned and let it drift off. He heard footsteps overhead. "Someone's coming."

"Now come on Cuz, let's just finish this thang and get o're to Gacy's, I'll buy the first round."

"You're buyin' all the beer tonight Craig, I want to get drunk enough to not remember today, and if'n we don't finish before dusk, I'll be waitin' on you ta get there."

"We'll finish up, start diggin."

"Hey! Hey! Can you hear me up there? I'm not dead! I'm alive! I'm alive! I can hear you," the new guy pleaded.

Monty heard the unmistakable scratch and thud of dirt being shoveled onto the casket.

"Hey, come on. Let me out of here. I'm alive. I'm alive! Please, let me out! HELP!"

"WOOOOOOOOOOOAH! WOOOOOOOOOAH!" Fremont moaned.

"Hey Craig, did you hear something?"

"Now Cuz, don't be startin' that again. Just keep shoveling."

"I swears I hear something."

"It ain't nothin' but the wind."

"WOOOOOOOOOAH! WOOOOOOOOOAH!

"Let me out! HEEEEEELLLLLPPPPP!" he screamed.

The shoveling stopped. "I swear I heard something that time."

"HEEEEELLLLLPPPP!" he shouted again.

"Craig, I hear something, something coming from this casket."

"HEEEELLLLPP! I'm here, I'm alive, there's been a mistake. I'm NOT DEAD!" he shouted.

"There ain't nothing coming from that casket, Cuz."

"I swear on my momma's grave, if you're jackin' with me, I'm gonna take this shovel and bop you 'cross the head and bury you right here, long with this dude."

"Come on Cuz, there's nothin' here but dead people, 'specially this guy."

"Why, who's this guy?"

"This here's Jerry Nimitz. You didn't read about it in the papers?"

"Nah, I don't never read no papers, too depressing."

"He's the shoe salesman from the Shoe Circus."

"What, did he get mobbed by a bunch of women at a shoe sale, like they was all fighting over the last pair of size eights?"

"Nah, some freak accident, he was gettin' a pair of pumps off the top shelf for this lady and he lost his balance and fell off the ladder."

"Ah, he fell off a ladder, that sucks."

"Yeah, but it gets worse, he landed on his back and all these shoe boxes fell on top of him."

"Guy got crushed by a bunch of women's shoes?"

"Nah, it gets worse. One of the shoe boxes that fell on him had a pair of stiletto heels."

"Ouch, that had to hurt."

"Yeah, but it gets worse, and this is the freaky part, one of the shoes came out of the box and the heel went right through his throat."

"Oh man."

"Yeah, this other shoe clerk went back to get some lady a pair of two-tone penny loafers and found him on the ground gasping for air. By the time the medics got there, he was dead."

"Ah, that's terrible."

"Store manager said it was a tragedy but they had their best day ever. He said they was gonna have a shoe sale in his honor."

"AHHH, that's nice."

"Hey, hey, I'm not dead, I'm down here, there's been a mistake, I'm still alive!" Jerry shouted.

"Tap that mound down a little, Cuz."

"HEY! HEY! Don't do that, come on man, let me out! I'm still alive!"

"Did you hear that Cuz?"

" I didn't hear nothin'."

The patting of the earth by the two men echoed through the grave like the closing of giant wooden door, the sound of their footsteps leaving like the sound of the key slipping from the lock of the dungeon door.

"Hey! Hey! Is anybody out there? Hey? Hey!" Jerry shouted.

"Wooooah. HEY NIM-NUTS! VEL-COM TO THE SIM-A-TARY." Fremont moaned slow and low.

"Who's there? What's going on?"

Jerry whined for hours and Fremont soon tired of messing with him. Finally Fremont shouted, "Hey Nimnuts, shut the hell up!"

The shoe salesman stifled a cry and sobbed quietly in his casket. Monty felt the coolness of the night and listened to the calming chirp of crickets.

Later, Monty felt the warmth from the surrounding soil, it must be midday, he sensed the thickness of the darkness had changed. The new neighbor had cried since early morning, bringing on another tirade from Fremont. He still hadn't figured it out.

The sirens started later. From far off they all felt a pressure in the air, a change they felt before they heard the screams. Nimnuts sensed it too and finally got the nerve to ask.

"What's that?" he asked. "What's that sound? Are they coming for me?"

"No one's coming for you Nimnuts," Fremont said. The siren screams got closer. The pitch was high and steady; everyone could feel the pain of these dead through their unending screams. Even Fremont cringed in his coffin at their unimaginable wakening.

"Are those sirens coming?" Nimnuts asked.

"No, new residents for Pine Hills Cemetery," Evan said and was drowned out by the screams. The sirens were the screams of pain, horrific, unending pain. The voices raw, insane.

"What is it?" Nimnuts tried to shout over the deafening cries. He got no reply. They were all silent in their graves, clinched and cringing in the knowledge of the sound. The screams passed and faded and still no one spoke. They could still hear the steady painful screams long after the cars departed.

"What is that!?" Nimnuts screamed, the cries getting to him.

"It's the ashes of the cremated," Evan said, "on their way to the mausoleum."

"You mean they can feel...they can feel the flames?" Nimnuts asked.

"Just like you will feel the worms," Fremont said.

"Just like you, Nimnuts, you awaken from death, and have this awareness, sense hot and cold, pain, boredom, for them...for them they will feel fire until they fade and are forgotten," Evans said.

"Yeah, unless you're famous, like ole Monty there, then you will scream forever," Fremont said.

"Shut up," Monty said.

Fremont laughed. "Just think, the feel of the fire on your skin, the burn in your bones and then, if you go to Hell, this is just the beginning."

"Lighten' up Fremont," Evans said.

"Pun! Pun!" Fremont shouted.

"Shut up Fremont," Monty shouted.

"My bodies burnin', I'm on fire," Fremont said in his best Elvis.

"Fremont, give it a rest," Evan said

"You said Monty's famous?" Nimnuts asked.

"You've never heard of Monty Compton?" Fremont asked.

"No," Nimnuts said.

"Evan, can you believe this guy, what, did you live in a box?" Fremont said.

"Monty's old school, kids these days listen to rap and crap like that," said Evan.

"Monty Compton, crooner to kings, lover of women, lots and lots of women. Ten ex-wives and more ex-lovers than you could ever count."

"Shut up Fremont," Monty said, Fremont laughed and stopped.

"Old Monty sang with Frankie and Sammy and Dino and all those guys. You have heard of Frank Sinatra and Sammy Davis, Jr. haven't you?" Fremont asked.

"Sure, who hasn't," Evan said.

"Well, Monty here was one of them guys, 'cept he was too busy getting laid to make the papers," Fremont said. "He cut three albums back in the 50's, made him rich and famous. Three-eyed Monty they used to call him, his dick was more famous than his voice."

"Hadn't you ever heard 'Our Love Will Last Forever'?" Evan asked.

"Ah, yeah, that old Hooligan's song," Nimnuts said.

"Nah, that's all Monty, he wrote that. Those one hit wonders couldn't play three chords between them," Fremont said.

"Wow, that's cool," Nimnuts said. "So, you were famous?"

"He was the most famous, world traveler, number one with the women, rich, guests of presidents and their wives," Fremont said.

"Shut up Fremont," Monty said for the millionth time.

"He sang with Sammy, Frank and Dean," Evan said

"The Brat Pack?" Nimnuts said.

"The Rat Pack, Nimnuts," Fremont said.

"He put the Rat in the Pack," Evan said.

"He taught them Cats to croon," Fremont said.

"A real celebrity?" said Nimnuts.

"Why do you think he's here?" Fremont said.

"Cause he's dead?" Nimnuts said.

"No, why do you think he's still here, awake," Evan said.

"I don't know, cause he's famous?" Nimnuts said.

"You got it Sherlock," Fremont said. "He'll be awake a long time."

"What about me?" Nimnuts asked.

"What about you, Nimnuts?" Fremont asked.

"What's going to happen to me?"

"Ha, how old's your mother?" Fremont asked.

"Seventy-two."

"You won't last 2 months after she dies," Fremont said.

"Hey Monty, tell him 'bout Chicago, you know, the three blondes," Fremont said and so it went, the coolness of the night, the heat of the day, the endless darkness, the incessant boredom, and time went slowly by. Time was immeasurable, the residents of Pine Hill Cemetery could not count the days, mark the time with scratches on the wall, no real discernable way to tell the passing of day into night and back into day.

"Hey new guy, what's your name?" Fremont asked. The diggers had just turned the dirt on another casket. The new guy woke with a scream.

"Did you hear that?" one of the diggers asked.

"Heard what?" the other said.

"That, dude. That. Don't you hear that, sounds like a scream," the digger said.

"Don' t you start talkin' like that again. I swear-ta-gawd you start hearin' stuff and I ain't never coming back with you again, I'll flip burgers 'fore I turn no more dirt on no more dead people."

"Ok, I'm joshin' ya, I don't hear nothing."

"Damn straight you ain't hearin' nothing," he said and patted the earth down. Their voices trailed as they left.

The new guy's screams carried through the packed soil of the graveyard and his awakening was long and painful.

"Hey, new guy! New guy! Shut Up!" Fremont shouted, there was no way to block the screams.

"What! Who's there?" the new guy said.

"What's your name?" Evan asked.

"Who's that? Who said that? HELP! Get me out of here!" he shouted.

Word came on the wind and the whispers told of the passing of Nimnut's mother at age 78. She was buried at Woodland Lawn, an unkempt cemetery on the north side with weeds more plentiful than flowers and most of the headstones had been removed by vandals and never replaced.

"Hey Nimnuts! Nimnuts!" Fremont shouted. There was no reply. "Hey, anyone heard from Nimnuts?"

"No," Evan said, "Nimnuts started fading the day after his mom died. He could barely talk yesterday. I bet he's gone."

"It never takes long after mamma goes," Fremont said. The cemetery sat silent the rest of the day. Someone had finally passed, to what, no one knew. They all hoped it was to somewhere better.

Evan faded and was gone, forgotten and his bones finally sat silent in his grave.

"Evan, hey Evan," Fremont said, his voice was hoarse and little more than a whisper. "I think Evan's finally gone too, lucky bastard."

Monty could barely hear him. "I think you're fading too," he said. "Fremont.

Fremont!" and with that, Fremont was gone. Monty was alone in his little corner of the cemetery and the time passed even more slowly. Monty lay in his grave with his memories, his triumphs and regrets and no ability to recreate or remedy any of them. This had to be Hell he thought. As in life, there were no answers to his questions, no one who could explain, there was only the gossip on the wind.

He often passed the time humming his old songs to himself, and noticed his voice was fading, his tunes were muffled. "Am I fading?" he said to himself, his voice barely a whisper. His limbs felt lighter, his memory fading, his head foggy like a champagne drunk and he floated in and out of awareness, he could feel the steady passing of time with the rhythm of hot and cold of the soil. He seemed to doze in and out of consciousness as he felt the cemetery soil warm and cool throughout the days.

He wandered in his thoughts and heard the whispers of the wind, calling his name. "Monty…" it said in a far away voice, beckoning him to come, "Monty…" it said more loudly this time.

"Monty was the greatest," someone shouted. "The King of the Crooners," the voices said directly above him.

"Monty, we love you," a female voice said. "Listen," she said.

Monty became aware that the words he heard were not the wind but voices above, mortals.

"Monty, they're playing your song," the girl said.

Monty heard a click and then his voice boomed loudly from the radio.

"In memory of the 50th anniversary of the untimely death of Monty Compton, W-H-E-L is producing a three day retrospective of the work of the King of Crooners," the DJ said in a deep and flowing voice.

"It's your music Monty, your music is being re-released and the world will stand and remember you again," the female said. "I am your biggest fan!"

Monty felt his mind and body pulled, as if from a deep sleep and tossed recklessly into the land of the living.

And as he heard the smooth, cool vocals lilting through the radio into the world, the song that had made him famous would be heard by millions and millions and he would be famous again, and he let out a long and painful scream, the scream of birth. The noise scared the two fans and they dropped the radio and ran off. Their story would attract thousands of fan worshipers and sightseers to his grave. He would feel them trample overhead and hear his songs over and over again. Forever famous he screamed, Forever Famous.

XIII

SNIPPETS

Snippets are really short stories that didn't take
a long time to write and won't take long to read.

SNIPPETS

▼

1

ROAD KILL

Kenneth Craddock sped down the back country road to Salamander Pass. Lulu would be waiting for him at the Lizard Lounge, but she would not wait long. He cursed the tiny, rented Volkswagen Beatle churned slowly around the bends without much power.

Ken was a large man with big, rough hands that clutched the tiny steering wheel. Hank of Hanks Handy Hardware had kept him late, trying to negotiate a few more cents off the cases of nuts and bolts that Ken tried to sell him. Cheap bastard, he got quantity discounts on shit-sized orders just because he'd been a customer for so long, but he never let up. Guy still drove a 20 year old truck, probably had the first buck he ever earned.

Ken was startled back to the road by the splat of a large bug against the windshield. "Got me another one," he said aloud. The windshield was being pelted by insect goo at dusk, he loved the sound of their tiny bodies hitting the windshield leaving colorful patterns of odd yellows, reds and greens. A large dragonfly struck the windshield and lodged beneath a wiper blade, its large bug eyes stared at him, seemed to plead with him for some sort of mercy, its fragile wing flopped a last good bye before it blew off. Another got stuck in the windshield wiper and Ken watched as the wind slowly bent the body into odd angles before ripping it apart. Ken turned on the wipers to shake of the bug's decapitated body off but all it did was spread the bug juice across the windshield and he couldn't see.

He pressed the washer button and it liquefied the mess and he was driving blind down the winding roads. He felt a bump, heard a loud thud that was the unmistakable sound of steel meeting bone and muscle. He looked in his rearview mirror and saw a raccoon thrashing around on the highway in the dying light.

"Ten points," he shouted. Damn, he loved that feel, that sound, there was nothing like it. He crossed a long bridge and bugs peppered his windshield like bb's, some soft like sand, the larger ones popping like small rocks.

He looked at his watch, 7 p.m. another thirty minutes of dusk and bug stew, and only 45 minutes before Lulu would go to another bar to find someone to keep her company and buy her drinks for the rest of the night. He stepped on the gas and turned on his high beams. The bright lights attracted bugs and small varmints. He swerved to the left and rolled over a large turtle crossing the road, it made a crunching sound he could hear clearer in the tiny VW, a feeling he didn't get in his four-wheel drive Dodge truck.

The road ahead was closed off, blocked by a Detour sign. Ken cursed his luck, paused and pulled a flask from his briefcase and took a drink of whisky and followed the sign to the left. How much time would this cost him he wondered. This road was curvier than the other and he turned off the radio, stepped on the pedal and sped into the curvy road. The rocking motion of the car eased his anxiety and he listened to the splatter of bugs on the windshield.

He saw an armadillo in the road, frozen, its eyes reflecting in the headlights and he pressed the pedal down and thought it funny how it too made a crunching sound, similar to the turtle. He swerved back and forth around the curves and saw the carcasses of dead animals on the road. A dog here and there, coons, foxes; a fuzzy hump that was probably a squirrel; buzzard feathers flapped in the wind from the crushed body stuck to the road, becoming road kill while feasting on victims of highway traffic.

This was treacherous road, the blind and curvy roads became death traps for unsuspecting critters and cars. He noticed an old Volvo crashed into a tree, the windows broken and the grass growing high, it had been there a while. He saw the smatterings of more animal carcasses and cars along the road, he struck two more animals along the way, a mangy dog and another armadillo, this was the most road kill he'd ever accumulated in one stretch of road.

He passed more dead animals, parts and pieces and found more cars rusting on the side of the road. He passed a VW beetle in the ditch upside down looking like a giant, stranded armadillo. He rounded a curve and saw a deer in the middle of the road, a large buck with a big rack, he sped up, the animal did not move, a 10+ buck was the ultimate trophy, he wished he had his truck. He sped up and moved to the center stripe, barreling down on top of the defenseless deer.

Ken didn't see the giant, hairy fist come out of the trees, he only heard the crunch of metal as the roof caved in, just yards from the deer. Ken felt the car lift into the air like a carnival ride and he tumbled upside down before he felt the bottom of the car being ripped out. A long finger, as big as a tree trunk swooped him out of the car and he watched the little yellow beetle crash next to a curve in the ditch when it fell. He saw stars and he turned and twisted and saw the cavernous jaws of the beast before experiencing that feeling of falling down the gullet of the beast.

Meetchum Butterfield cursed at the detour sign, he had thirty minutes to get the lumber office to make his insurance pitch. He hated these back road hicks but they had money and the lumber yard was one of the biggest employers in the area.

He sped up through the curves, oblivious to all the road kill that littered the highway.

SNIPPETS

▼

2

STRESSED

Well, it's done. I did it, I've set my place in history with a…well, historical decision, and proved to the world I am a man, and they said I was wishy-washy he laughed. They said I was weak, couldn't make decisions. I showed them. I will show them all. You can't push me around, no sirree. Can't push me around anymore. Red bastards think they can sit there and trash me all the time and me to take it. Not gonna happen, not gonna take their B.S anymore.

"Are you talking to me?" Warren said into the mirror.

He looked away slowly over his right shoulder at the bed, then quickly back at himself in the mirror.

"Are you talking to me?" he said and turned to face the mirror straight on.

"Cause if you're talking to me, you're talking to this," he said slowly reaching behind him with his right hand and then jerking it around in the deadly L-shape of a gun. He pointed his index finger/barrel at the mirror and cocked his thumb with his left hand while making a ratcheting sound through his teeth. He lowered his voice, deep and monotone, and in his best Eastwood voice said:

"I know what you're thinking, punk, did he fire 5 shots or 6." He nodded at himself in the mirror. "To tell you the truth, in all the excitement, I don't remember, so tell me Punk, do you feel lucky?"

"BANG! BANG! BANG! BANG!" he shouted and shot imaginary bullets into imaginary foes. "I shot them all you stinkin' Commies."

Warren stared at himself in the mirror, he didn't look too intimidating in his white and black striped boxers and sleeveless "wife beater" t-shirt, maybe it was the black socks that made him look dorky. His face was old, this job had aged him. His skin hung loose and pale from his weary bones and he was losing all his hair. He had been such a dashing man in his youth.

A sudden, aggressive knock at the door sent Warren behind a chair.

"Sir, I have an urgent phone call for you," the voice on the other side said.

He crouched behind the chair, shaking.

"Sir? Sir, did you hear me? I have an urgent phone call for you, it's the Vice President."

Warren looked around the room, trying to think. What to do…what to say…

"Tell him I'm not here."

"What?"

"Tell him I'm not here."

"Ah, that doesn't work anymore, sir."

"Tell him I've requested not to be disturbed."

"Sir, he says it is very urgent."

"Do as I say!" Warren shouted, standing up from behind the chair.

Silence from the other side of the door. It's good to be king he thought to himself. He uncocked his gun/thumb and put it back into his imaginary holster. It was 8 a.m. Two hours till operation Freedom Belch.

He sat on the couch with a Scotch and lit a cigarette. One year, 4 months and 15 days until retirement. Could he make it? Warren wasn't sure if the man in the mirror could. He looked so frail. He was so tired. He couldn't wait to get out, get away from the stress, the long hours, the politics; all the back stabbing and lies and deceits, all the hypocrisy, and ties, he hated wearing ties.

Living under a microscope, under the white hot spotlight all the time, it got old. It took its toll on a fellow. You don't really know what you're getting into until it's too late. He paced around the room and stared out the window onto the lawn. It's not like they have classes for this either, it's all OJT, on the job training. Sink or swim. He felt a mind-numbing headache starting, like a giant hand squeezing his tiny brain until it bled.

Oh God, was he bleeding? Warren didn't feel any leaks from his ears or nose and he clamped his teeth tightly together to keep his brain from crashing through his skull. He stumbled to the night stand and pulled open the drawer. He searched around frantically inside for his pills and dry swallowed 3 Vicodins. He lay on the couch and squeezed his eyes shut against the stress headache and waited for it to pass.

The pounding on the door woke him again.

"Sir, it's very urgent, the Secretary of Defense and Vice President is here, sir, they are demanding to come in."

"Tell them I've gone to the movie store, tell them I had a late fee," he said.

"Sir, they insist it's a matter of national security," the man said.

"Oh, Sergeant, they always say that, tell them I have a headache and don't wish to be disturbed."

The Sergeant left and he heard a heated argument at the end of the hallway.

Sometimes you have to make tough decisions, throw sand in the face of the bully, tell them enough's enough. He opened the briefcase and fingered the red button he had pressed an hour earlier. Bombs away! "To Russia with Love" he snickered.

SNIPPETS

▼

3

SCIENCE EXPERIMENT

Jennifer knocked at the door of Ray's apartment and got no answer. She saw his car parked crooked in the parking lot and knocked again, then pounded on the door before she heard the uncertain shuffle of someone inside.

"Open up," she said.

"What do you want?" It was Ray's voice on the other side of the door, hoarse and irritable.

"We're supposed to be at study group 15 minutes ago," she said. Her biology grades were bad and sinking fast and she needed to pass. Ray's parents paid for everything and he was on the six year degree plan. He wasn't so concerned with biology or any other class.

"Come on, open up or I'm leaving," she said. She heard the chain lock come off the lock and the door peeked open. Ray was standing in his underwear, blocking the sunlight with his arm. He stepped back and Jennifer pushed through.

The apartment smelled of stale beer and sweat. She let her eyes adjust to the darkness and flipped on a light switch. Ray had stumbled back to the couch and was cussing about the intensity of the lamps.

"Shut up, we have to get to group, you know I need this grade," she said.

"You go on, I don't feel good," Ray said, pulling a blanket over his head.

Jennifer walked towards him and stumbled over a pizza box, the apartment was filthy, pizza boxes littered the room, some filled with half eaten pizza and crushed beer cans, ashtrays overflowed on every table. The room stunk.

"Get me some water," Ray said.

Jennifer glared at the covered heap and then weaved around the scattered trash to the kitchen. The sink was piled high with beer mugs, dirty dishes, old spaghetti stuck to the plates like dried worms. Flies buzzed around the kitchen, sampling the fraternity buffet. Jennifer opened the refrigerator looking for bottled water or a non-alcoholic canned drink. No luck on any account.

The first thing that struck her was the smell, awful. Plates of food and opened plastic dishes were strewn about on the shelves, plates stacked on one another. Spaghetti hung like red crusted strings through the wired shelves. Black mold covered the plates like a fuzzy carpet. She slammed the door, refusing to reach into the giant Petri dish.

"That's just nasty, Ray, it looks like a science experiment in there," she said and heard the pop of a beer can behind her.

Ray sat on the edge of the couch in his underwear wearing sunglasses and held a beer in his hand. She glared at him again.

"Hair of the dog," he said and toasted her.

"What is that crap in the refrigerator? You need to clean this place up," she said.

Ray let out a long, loud belch.

"You're disgusting," she said and walked out. She had to study, she was on a limited scholarship and had to pass all of her classes and didn't have time to hang out with losers.

Ray stood at the patio window and watched her drive off as he peed into the big planter. He gulped his warm beer down and stumbled to the refrigerator in hopes of finding a cold one. He reached in and fished around and wrapped his hands around a cold can, it was slimy. Budweiser! He wiped the food crusts and slime from off the top and popped it open and sucked it down. His eyes were finally able to focus, it was 9 a.m.

He pondered that for a moment and remembered biology study group, 'oh well, third time's a charm,' he said under his breath. He'd need to drop the class again, pre-med was not going well for him, maybe video game design would be better he said and turned on the TV and plugged in a Mario Brothers game. He kept his shades on because the light still hurt his eyes.

After Mario fell to his death three times, Ray felt he needed another beer, a warm six-pack sat in the box at his feet, cold ones could be chilling in the fridge. Hot and here, cold and there? Cold won out and he spun the beer wheel of chance and wandered into the kitchen, the flies dashed around the room, getting bolder. He opened the door and fished around for cold can, bottle, any alcoholic container. The light was burned out so he fished around in the dark and clasped a cold can and then something bit him, hard, like a spider or a snake. He dropped the can and pulled his hand out quickly, blood oozed from two holes in his hand between his thumb and forefinger. It hurt. He stepped back and grabbed a dirty dish towel and wrapped his hand to stop the bleeding.

He looked into the fridge, it was dark. He flipped on the kitchen light and removed his shades and peered in. Spaghetti hung like jungle snakes from the shelves and black mold seemed to have taken over the inside, covering the plates and walls of the ice box. The fuzzy black mold seemed to shimmer and pulse. He peered in and saw the cold beer can and reached quickly in and grabbed it before anything could bite him again.

Successful, he played two more games and fell asleep. He woke up a few hours later with a headache. The room was stifling hot, the A/C off. A foul odor filled the room. He wiped his face with his hand and it tickled. Looking down he saw his hand was covered in black mold, fuzzy and pulsing. He screamed and jumped up and slipped on the black mold that covered the ground.

Black mold snaked from the refrigerator and covered the floors and the walls and had inched up his legs. He jumped up and stumbled and fell into the sticky mold that held him like fly paper. He felt the fuzzy mold crawl over him and devoured him before he could scream.

After two days the mold consumed everything in the room, furniture, electrical cords, plastic and fabric turned into mush and collapsed under the weight of the back mold. Jennifer knocked on his door three days later and left after she got no answer. Rene, the apartment manager came by two weeks later after the rent was late and found the apartment abandoned, cleaned out of everything. She would keep the deposit as the tenant had repainted the walls and redone the floors in a dark shag carpet. The room felt so alive and although unusual was tastefully done.

SNIPPETS

▼

4

CRACK BABY

Crystal wore a loose fitting t-shirt to hide her belly, the baby was due next month and she would prefer people think she was fat rather than pregnant. She stood in the ally and pulled the jacket tight around her, the wind bit right through her and she was shaking. An intercom system beside the door blared static and an unhappy voice said, "What?"

"It's me, Crystal, let me up, it's cold out here," she said pressing the intercom button.

There was a long pause, "what do you want Crystal?" the voice asked.

"You know, come on, let me in," she pleaded.

"Did you have that baby?" the voice asked.

Crystal didn't answer right away, she huddled in her jacket and looked both ways down the alley, it was vacant.

She pressed the intercom button and said, "No."

"Well get out of here Crystal, I told you last time I wasn't going to sell you nothing more 'till that baby was out," the voice said.

"Ah, come on Spider, I'm hurtin', I need something, just a little taste to get me through. My old man kicked me out again, I ain't got nowhere to go," she said, her nose running, tears welled up in her eyes.

Another long pause. She waited for an answer.

"Come on Spider, please," she said, her hands aching from the cold as she pressed the intercom button.

"You got any money?" Spider asked.

She paused, she had none. "Ah, no Spider, come on, for old times' sake, I'm hurtin'," she pleaded, "you know I can still perform."

"Shit, not with no pregnant bitch," Spider said.

She winced at the rejection. "Come on Spider, you know I got other talents, make you feel real good," Crystal said, shaking in her coat, the desperation growing quickly, she had no place else to go and nobody who might take her offer.

She felt a big sense of relief when the door buzzed open. She climbed the stairs slowly. She was 7 months pregnant and the baby already weighed 8 pounds, she struggled up the stairs, stepping past junkies laying motionless in a drug haze on the steps. She knocked on the door of apartment 413 hoping Spider wouldn't challenge her anymore. The door opened slowly and she saw Spider sitting in the center of the curved couch group surrounded by four guys and two girls, they were all smoking crack and large, rolled joints, the air was thick with dope. She glanced at them and looked down, not wanting to make eye contact.

"Hey everybody, look who's here, it's Crystal, her momma loved the stuff so much, she named her daughter after the drug," Spider said in grand style.

Spider had his arm around a girl in a pink halter top; her arms were covered in colorful tattoos. "Is that your real name?" she asked.

Crystal glanced up at her and quickly back to Spider. "Hey Spider, I need some help, real bad."

Spider's face got serious, "I thought I told you I didn't want to see you 'fore that bambino had hatched," he said.

"I know Spider, I'm trying, I just can't, Roger kicked me out…"

"Why, cause you was street walkin' and druggin' again weren't you?" Spider said.

"Ah, well, you know Spider, I got to make a living," she said.

"When's the last time you ate?" he asked.

"Well, you know Spider, I don't really remember, a while. I know it's been a while since I had a hit though, I can feel it, Junk can feel it, he gets real restless when he's straight, he goes through withdrawal, same as the rest of us," she said.

"You mean you're pregnant?" the girl in pink asked through a fog of pot.

"Yeah, she hides it well," Spider said.

"You named your baby Junk?" one of the other girl's asked.

"Yeah, cause that's what she likes," Spider said, "she could have called it Crack or Dick for that matter," and they all laughed at her.

"Hey Spider, come on, can I have a hit, a little taste, I'm really hurtin" she pleaded.

"I can't believe you're doing drugs while pregnant," the girl in pink said.

"Shit, she was druggin' when she got pregnant and never stopped," Spider said.

"That's fucked up," said one of the guys in an Army jacket. He let out a big bloom of meth smoke.

Crystal was getting anxious, Junk was turning somersaults in her belly, kicking the sides of her uterus and she had to pee real bad. He whole body was twitching. She stared at the crack pipes being passed around.

"Come on Spider, please," she said.

"Ok," he said and Crystal nearly shouted and took a step toward the group.

"After you do him," Spider said, pointing to the guy in the Army jacket.

"What?" she said.

"Come on Crystal, show Dylan some of your talents, you said you would," Spider said.

She looked over at Dylan, he was skinny and gaunt, a large pointed nose protruded over an unshaved face. He looked at her with a little disgust.

"Spider, you know," she stammered.

"You said you had no money, no money, no nookie, no drugs baby, shit ain't changed," Spider said and blew out smoke from his joint.

"I don't even know him," she said.

"When the Hell did that ever stop you from anything?" asked.

"I said I'd do you Spider, you know, old times' sake," she said.

"I ain't doin' no pregnant crack whore, Be-Atch," he said and leaned over and kissed the young, skinny girl in the pink halter top on the shoulder.

"Go on," Spider said, he held up the crack pipe, if you want some of this, you gotta do him."

Dylan looked barely conscious. She hesitated but her body ached and twitched and Junk was pounding on her stomach. She needed some medicine real bad.

"Do it, do it, do it," they all chanted.

Crystal got on her knees and crawled over to the stoned out Dylan. He didn't even notice as she undid his pants.

"Do it, do it," they chanted in the background.

Junk kicked her hard in the stomach and she felt something rip. Dylan's eyes got big and he started to scream as long claws tore out of Crystal's stomach. A deformed head appeared, lidless, misshapen eyes off center bugged out at him, the baby snarled and drooled through a mouth that was far too big for the face, sharp teeth snapped and he snorted through unformed cartilage that was its nose. Dylan could not move, Crystal had him pinned to the couch and as the baby tore its way through her stomach she quickly bled out and died in his lap.

The baby leapt at Dylan's face and tore into his drug soaked brain with long, sharp fingernails, feasting on the blood and the man-made crystals that circulated there. All Spider could do is watch in horror and the drug starved monster ate through his friend.

The girls were screaming and when Junk had finished slurping out the goo in Dylan's head, he turned and charged the girls. It nearly reached Spider's girlfriend when it was pulled back by the umbilical cord and it was yanked backwards and it tumbled to the ground. It growled and leaped again, this time it ripped loose of Crystal's stomach, freeing itself from the fat red placenta. The umbilical cord whipped around and wrapped around the girl's throat and the frayed end darted into her neck and began draining her drug soaked blood from her body. It feasted and the hunger only intensified, it craved more and when all the druggies in the room were dead, Junk crawled onto the couch and slept.

Later, Junk awoke, his whole body twitching, instinct told him he needed to feed and the naked pink monstrosity, slipped out of the window in search of blood and drugs.

THE FEAR

▼

A PLAY IN ONE ACT

BY

EMMITTE HALL

THIS PLAY WAS FIRST PRESENTED AT TYLER CIVIC
THEATRE'S THIRD ANNUAL FESTIVAL OF PLAYS IN
TYLER, TEXAS.

"THE FEAR"

SETTING

PLACE: GRANDPA WILLIS' HOMESTEAD, A REMOTE CABIN IN THE WOODS. THE ACTION TAKES PLACE IN THE MAIN ROOM OF THE CABIN, A COMBINATION LIVING ROOM, KITCHEN, DINING ROOM. IT IS CROWDED WITH A DINNING TABLE; AN OLD, DATED, COUNTRY STYLE COUCH; A MATCHING OVERSTUFFED CHAIR; A ROUGH-WOOD COFFEE-TABLE; A ROCKING CHAIR. A MASSIVE, GRAY ROCK FIREPLACE IS IN THE MIDDLE OF THE BACK WALL, THERE ARE STACKS OF 4 FOOT, SLENDER STAKES, EACH SHARPENED TO A POINT, ON EACH SIDE OF THE FIREPLACE. THE PLACE HAS A CLUTTERED, UNKEPT AIR ABOUT IT. THERE ARE DOORS LEADING OFF STAGE INTO THE BACKDOOR, BATHROOM AND BEDROOM. THERE IS A FRONT PORCH WITH A WINDOW LOOKING OUT.

Time
The present; a fall evening, crisp and cold.

CAST OF CHARACTERS

GRANDPA WILLIS-Big guy, 60's, worn, bib-overalls and dirty t-shirt; large, rough hands. He has worked hard all of his life.

MATT-Grandpa Willis'grandson. A broke college student, wearing jeans and a t-shirt. His hair is straggly and he has not shaven in a few days.

NANCY-Matt's former girlfriend-pretty Goth chick dressed all in black, with black lipstick and black nail polish, about Matt's age.

SHERIFF GRAYSON-County Sheriff. Middle-aged, big guy in uniform with a gun and a gut, he knows everybody in the county.

STAGE IS DARK

Lights up on GRANDPA WILLIS walking around in circles in center of the living room. He has a large hunting knife that he is using to sharpen one of the stakes. He is grumbling to himself. MATT steps onto the front porch and knocks loudly.

GRANDPA
Who's there?

MATT
It's me Grandpa, open up.

GRANDPA
Who's me?

MATT
Your grandson, Matt. Come on,
it's cold out here.

GRANDPA
Matt's dead.

MATT
Quit kidding, I'm fine.

GRANDPA

(GRANDPA opens the door, pointing the stake at MATT'S chest)

Who are you?

MATT
It's me, Matt.

GRANDPA
Matt's dead.

MATT
I'm not dead Grandpa.

GRANDPA

If you're not dead, where you been?

MATT

(MATT slides in around GRANDPA and his pointed stake.)

I went to college, remember?

GRANDPA

Nah, Matt disappeared four years ago and I don't know who the hell you are.

MATT

Ah, come on Gramps, I know it's been a while…

GRANDPA

Four years, it's been four years since they drug poor Matt into the mines.

MATT

I wasn't drug anywhere. You know I would never go down there.

GRANDPA

People go into the mines but they don't come out.

MATT

(sadly)

I know Grandpa.

GRANDPA

How do I know you're not one
of them?

MATT

One of who?

GRANDPA

One of them,(pause) A Feeder.

MATT

A what?

GRANDPA

(Shouting, aggressive with the stake)

Scourge! Monster! Flesh eating
beast from Hell! Get thee out
of Matt's body!

MATT

Grandpa, it is me. I'm ok.
I'm back.

GRANDPA

Back from the dead?

MATT

Back from Lexington.

GRANDPA

(GRANDPA still holds the stake defensively and approaches MATT closer so he can see MATT'S face better)

You do kinda favor my grandson.

MATT

Come on Gramps, you remember?
I went off to school. You gave
me your old truck.

GRANDPA

The Dodge truck?

MATT

Yeah, the diesel with the
rusted out bed.

(GRANDPA eyes him suspiciously, puts down the stake.)

MATT (CONT)

First gear didn't work.

GRANDPA

My old Dodge, so where is it?

MATT

What, the truck?

GRANDPA

Yeah, where's my truck?

MATT

It broke down two years ago
and I had to sell it.

GRANDPA

You sold my truck? I loved
that truck.

MATT

You said you hated that truck,
that's why you gave it to
me.

GRANDPA

It was my favorite truck, best
truck I ever had.

MATT

You never liked that truck.

GRANDPA

So, how'd you get here?

MATT

I took the bus.

GRANDPA

Bus don't stop in Draiden no
more.

MATT

Sure   it   does,   Greyhound
dropped me off at the station
downtown   and   guess   what,
Nancy was working the ticket
counter.

GRANDPA

Who's Nancy?

MATT

My   old   girlfriend,   (pause)
from high school.

GRANDPA

Nancy's dead.

MATT

She's not dead.

GRANDPA

She's dead, I miss my truck
and the bus don't stop here
no more.

MATT

She's not dead, Grandpa. She's
coming by later, you'll see.

GRANDPA

What's she comin' her for?

MATT

She invited me to a party, a
lot of my old friends will be
there.

GRANDPA

You can't go out after dark.

MATT

Probably because they roll up
the sidewalks at five.

GRANDPA

Nobody goes out in the night,
not in Draiden, not after
dark.

MATT

Cause there's nothing to do.

GRANDPA

Cause everyone's dead.

MATT
(sadly)
I'm sorry about Grandma.

GRANDPA

Sorry 'bout what?

MATT

That she died.

GRANDPA

Who told you that?

MATT

Aunt Bessie. She called and told me the funeral was tomorrow, so I jumped on the first bus I could get.

GRANDPA

Bessie told you that?

MATT

Yeah, she called yesterday.

GRANDPA

MMMM. That's strange.

MATT

What's strange?

GRANDPA

Grandma didn't die.

MATT

Grandma's still alive?

GRANDPA

No, she didn't die, she was murdered.

                    MATT
Murdered? Aunt Bessie didn't
say anything about her being
murdered.

                    GRANDPA
No, she wouldn't either.
Bessie's one of them.

                    MATT
One of who?

                    GRANDPA
The whole town's turned evil
Matt, they've all turned.

                    MATT
Turned? Into what?

                    GRANDPA
Feeders.

(There is a sudden loud, howling of wolves from all around the cabin. GRANDPA rushes to the window and looks out. MATT appears not to hear the wolves and does not react.)

                    GRANDPA (CONT)
Hear that? They're listening.

                    MATT
I don't hear anything.

                    GRANDPA
It's the creatures, they're
hungry. When you hear the
howling of the wolves, the
undead walk the earth in

search of blood. Someone will
die by dawn.

MATT

Huh?

GRANDPA

Something got loose from the
mines, something evil and it's
turned this town into a nest
of monsters.

MATT

What are you talking about?

GRANDPA

There's always been evil here.
You remember the tales?

MATT

Sure, everyone said the mines
were cursed.

GRANDPA

They weren't just stories,
Matt. Them mines have killed
a lot of people, lot of bodies
still down there. That much
death breeds evil.

MATT

(MATT unconsciously picks up
a stake and begins diddling
with it)
They were just stories,
Grandpa, old wives' tales.

GRANDPA

No, the ghosts of those early miners walk these woods.

MATT

Local legends, it sold a few books and souvenirs, that's all.

GRANDPA

Something evil lived here, old as the hills, dark as the caves. The graveyard's full of its victims.

MATT

Victims of what?

GRANDPA

The monster. You been ta the old cemetery?

MATT

Sure.

GRANDPA

'member those stones etched with the knotted cross?

MATT

Yeah, in the old part, all the headstones had that cross.

GRANDPA

It's a talisman, to make sure the dead stayed buried.

MATT

What?

GRANDPA

Them early settlers found the source of the evil, they captured it and put it ta the ground. They buried it in the mines then closed the tunnels.

MATT

Ok, so what's the problem?

GRANDPA

It got out.

MATT

How did that happen?

GRANDPA

When they opened the mines, your daddy and his crew found it.

MATT

When was that?

GRANPDA

'Member the night Jessup died?

MATT

Yeah.

GRANDPA

They was diggin' out the Widow Maker, the deepest of the old tunnels. At the end of that tunnel, they found this rock covered in strange symbols.

MATT

What kind of symbols?

GRANDPA

None of the crew knew, the
only thing they did recognize
was the knotted cross.

MATT

Like from the cemetery?

GRANDPA

Yeah, so they moved the rock
and found a chamber, 'bout the
size of this room, and inside
they found it.

MATT

Found what?

GRANDPA

The beast, the source of the
evil. They let it loose that
night and it's run loose in
Draiden ever since.

MATT

So what's this have to do with
Jessup?

GRANDPA

The beast killed him.

MATT

How do you know this?

GRANDPA

Night Jessup died, your daddy
came here. He was scared, real

scared. He told me about the
chamber and the beast they
found.

MATT

(shakes his head in disbelief)

GRANDPA

In the corner, a small creature
covered in long, gray hair.
They shown their flashlights
on it and it came at them,
snarling and lashing it's
teeth. Jessup was standing in
the doorway and the monster
bit into his neck and then
ran out into the mines. Jessup
died right there.

MATT

Dad said he fell into the
auger.

GRANDPA

That's   what   they   told
everybody. Who'd believe 'em?
Crew figured they'd be fired if
they started spreading stories
'bout monsters in the mines
and they all had families to
support, so they made up the
story about Jessup. They all
agreed to keep it secret.

MATT

Dad never said anything about monsters.

GRANDPA

'cause he was scared, didn't hardly believe it his self, but next shift, they saw Jessup in the tunnels.

MATT

I thought you said Jessup was dead.

GRANDPA

He was, but he came back. And every night after that, a miner was killed or came up missing.

MATT

And you think this monster was killing them?

GRANDPA

Not just the monster, but the army it created. All the victims come back as Feeders, undead creatures hungry for blood.

MATT

Grandpa, this is all hard to believe.

GRANDPA

The monster got out, and it's spreading death all over

Draiden, but I'm gonna kill
'em, I'm gonna rid this town
of all the monsters and I need
your help, Matt.

MATT

(There is a sudden, loud howling of wolves outside the cabin, GRANDPA reacts to it but MATT does not hear it)

Did you tell the Sherriff?

GRANDPA

He's one of them. He's not a
Feeder, not yet, but he don't
believe me, he's evil.

MATT

I didn't come home to kill
monsters, Grandpa.

GRANDPA

The monster killed your daddy.

MATT

What?

GRANDPA

It killed your daddy.

MATT

He died in a cave in.

GRANDPA

No, the monster got him in
the mines. I saw the body all
tore to shreds, it weren't no
cave in. But I got him 'fore
he could change.

MATT

What did you do, Grandpa?

GRANDPA

I put a stake through him, afore he turned into the likes that killed him, and on the roof of his casket, I painted a knotted cross. Your daddy rests in peace to this day.

MATT

You put a stake through your son's heart?

GRANDPA

(points to MATT'S stick)

Yep, just like that one.

MATT

(Matt drops the stick and retreats in horror)

GRANDPA

It's the only way, the only way to kill them things, keep 'em from coming back and thirsting for blood. Your grandma was murdered by one of them creatures too. You see what needs to be done?

MATT

No.

> **GRANDPA**
>
> We got to rid this town of
> them things, drive a stake
> through their heart, keep 'em
> from feeding, keep 'em from
> spreading their evil to other
> towns, Matt.

(There's a heavy knock at the door)

> **SHERIFF**
>
> Willis. Willis, it's Sheriff
> Grayson, need to talk to
> you.

> **GRANDPA**

(GRANDPA grabs a stake and opens the door, SHERIFF walks in and nods at MATT)

> What do you want?

> **SHERIFF**
>
> Put that down. I need to ask
> you about something.

> **GRANDPA**
>
> Well?

> **SHERIFF**
>
> Have you been to the morgue?

> **GRANDPA**
>
> No, why?

SHERIFF

(SHERIFF points at MATT)

Who's that?

GRANDPA

That's my grandson.

SHERIFF

Mathew?

GRANDPA

Yeah.

SHERIFF

Oh, I didn't recognize you, it's been a few years.

GRANDPA

What do you want, Sheriff?

SHERIFF

Someone's taken your wife's body from the morgue.

MATT

Somebody's taken Grandma's body? Why?

SHERIFF

We think it's just kids, Willis, some sick joke or something.

GRANDPA

It ain't no kids and you know it. Them creatures got her. They're gonna turn her into a Feeder.

SHERIFF

Now Willis, you can just turn that crazy talk off. Lot of people in town know your views about the mines and these monsters and all.

GRANDPA

There's something evil out there.

SHERIFF

I think some kids are playing a sick joke on you, playing on your paranoia. They've heard you talk about the monsters. When I catch who done it, they're going to be in a lot of trouble.

GRANDPA

I'm gonna deal out the trouble, Sherriff.

SHERIFF

Now Willis, you leave this to me. I know you want to put her in her final resting place tomorrow and I'll do everything I can to find her, I'm sorry.

GRANDPA

Sorry? You didn't have nothing to do with it did you?

SHERIFF
Look Willis, I know you've had some rough times since you lost your son in the mine...

GRANDPA
It's not the mine Sheriff, it's what come out of there.

SHERIFF
We're forming a search party at first light. You can meet us at the flag pole if you want.

GRANDPA
She's gone, Sheriff. She'll be one of them by morning.

SHERIFF
Willis, I don't have time for this today, I'm real sorry, and I'll do all I can. I'll find her, I promise.

(SHERIFF leaves, GRANDPA stares at him as he leaves and shuts the door. He turns and looks at MATT.)

GRANDPA
Do you see? Do you see now, that evil lives here? They got your grandma, Boy. What are you gonna do about it?

MATT
This is crazy, Grandpa. All this talk of monsters and vampires.

GRANDPA

Is it? This town's dying.

MATT

That's what little towns do, progress or die, change or turn into a ghost town.

GRANDPA

People are disappearing in the middle of the night, Matt, no word, no good-byes, leaving all their stuff behind. That ain't normal.

MATT

They're dying of boredom Gramps, there's nothing to do here, that's why they're leaving.

GRANDPA

Think about it, you got a big mining operation here, good payin' jobs.

MATT

Yeah. So?

GRANDPA

So, where're all the people?

MATT

All the people?

GRANDPA

The truck drivers, the delivery people, mechanics, where are

they? This town ought to be
thriving?

MATT

I guess so.

GRANDPA

How many people did you see
in town?

MATT

Not many?

GRANDPA

They all go home before dark,
not many people left.

MATT

Downtown did look kind of
sparse.

GRANDPA

There's nothing left, the
bike shop, the hobby store,
my hardware store, they're
all gone.

MATT

I think you can blame that on
Wal-Mart more than Dracula.

GRANDPA

If your daddy hadn't gone into
the mines, he might still be
here. He'd help me fight these
devils, cursed place.

MATT

It was the only job he could
get.

GRANDPA

He was doin' fine at the
hardware store.

MATT

The business was failing,
Grandpa, it wasn't your fault,
you just can't compete against
the big chain stores.

GRANDPA

It would've been his if he'd
lived.

MATT

I know; he loved working in
that store with you. That's
all he wanted to do, but the
business was failing.

GRANDPA

My grand daddy started that
store, and my dad run it,
just like I run it, like your
daddy could've and then it
would have been yours if you
wanted it.

MATT

That would have been nice,
but it didn't happen.

GRANDPA

Them mines killed him, whatever was down there killed him and now it's killin' this whole town, bit by bit.

MATT

So what is it Grandpa, ghosts or werewolves. Vampires, maybe a little voodoo?

GRANDPA

You don't believe me, do you?

MATT

You haven't said a sane thing since I got here.

GRANDPA

Oh yeah, you said Aunt Bessie called you.

MATT

Yeah.

GRANDPA

Bessie's been dead nine months.

MATT

What?

GRANDPA

I bought her tombstone, stood in the rain and watched them bury her.

MATT

How is that possible?

GRANDPA

She came back, Matt, she came back and she wants you. I seen her ghost, two weeks ago outside, in the mist, she was calling me to come out, to come out and join them.

MATT

What did you do?

GRANDPA

That night? I hid. Like a coward I hid in here with my shot gun. But that's when I decided this had to end. I had to rid this town of the monsters. This used to be good town, with good people, but it's changing, Matt. It's being taken over by evil.

MATT

So what are you going to do, kill everybody in town?

GRANDPA

That's the only way to keep it from spreading. I can't do it alone Matt, there's too many of them.

MATT

You want me to help? What? Our neighbors? My friends?

GRANDPA

It's the whole town, Matt. They all got evil in them now.

MATT

I don't know Grandpa.

GRANDPA

They got your grandma. She was good to you. We took you in when your dad died, gave you a roof, food, what money we could for school.

MATT

But you're talking about killing people, a lot of people.

GRANDPA

(GRANDPA hands MATT a sharpened stake)

They ain't people, Matt, they're unholy beasts that feed on the good folks of this town, the town you grew up in. They turn them into something undead, claiming more and more victims. I, by God am not going to stand by and let that happen. Are you with me Matt?

MATT

I don't know Grandpa?

(There's a knock at the door. GRANDPA looks at MATT and approaches the door with a pointed stake, ready to kill whoever or whatever is on the other side.)

                    GRANDPA
        Who's there?

                     NANCY
        Is Matt here?

                    GRANDPA

(peeks out the window)

                Oh my God, it's one of them,
                it's a Feeder and it's come
                for you Matt. Quick get me a
                stake.

(MATT picks up a stake and hand it to GRANDPA. GRANDPA hides behind the door and slowly opens it).

                     NANCY

(NANCY walks in carrying a beer can. She sees MATT but does not notice GRANDPA who is sneaking up behind her ready to drive a stake through her heart)

                Hey, Matt, how's it goin?

                     MATT
        Stop Grandpa! Don't.

(MATT steps in to keep GRANDPA from stabbing NANCY)

                  MATT (CONT)
        It's Nancy, remember, I told
        you about her, I saw her at

the bus station. Remember Grandpa, my old girlfriend from high school.

NANCY

Who you callin' old?

GRANDPA

Nancy?

MATT

Yeah, Grandpa, it's Nancy, Nancy Westermine, she's been here plenty of times, had dinner with us.

GRANDPA

(confused)

Nancy?   Little   Nancy Westermine?

MATT

Yes, Grandpa, don't you remember her?

GRANDPA

(disoriented)

I thought she was dead. I didn't… don't recognize her.

MATT

It's her Grandpa.

GRANDPA

Why's she look like (pause) like one of them?

NANCY

What's he mean I look like
one of them?

GRANDPA

Like one of the undead.

NANCY

Huh?

MATT

Grandpa thinks there's monsters
taking over Draiden.

NANCY

Kookie man.
          (to Matt)
I'd heard your grandpa had
lost it. Everyone in town says
he sees ghosts and stuff.

GRANDPA

What   happened   to   your
parents?

NANCY

My mom? She died.

GRANDPA

Are you sure?

NANCY

Am I sure she died?

GRANDPA

Are   you   sure   she   stayed
dead?

NANCY

(to MATT)

He's doin' the crazy talk again.

MATT

Grandpa thinks that something got out of the mine and has been killing people.

NANCY

What do you mean 'something got out.'

MATT

You remember all those ghost stories our parents told us as kids?

NANCY

Sure, same stories that our grandparents told their kids and same one's we'll tell ours.

GRANDPA

They're not just stories, Nancy. There's always been something evil here, 'cept now it's running loose.

NANCY

Are you talking about those stories of the ghosts of the miners and settlers?

MATT

There's always been stories about ghosts around here.

NANCY

Yeah, Old Miss Minter, lost in the winter

MATT

Come back dead and lookin for some sinners.

NANCY

Better not be you.

MATT

Jonathon Overmeyer, burned in a fire,

NANCY

Came back, hungry and charred.

MATT

You better hide.

NANCY

Freda Stout, got her eyes gouged out.

MATT

Came back blind, killin' everyone she finds.

NANCY

She better not find you.

GRANDPA

Those weren't just scary rhymes to keep you kids in line. They

were true. Something's evil
been here a long time.

NANCY

What, like the boogieman of
Draiden?

GRANDPA

People been disapperin' in
the night, just vanishing,
they're gone.

NANCY

They're getting the Hell out
of here, like Matt did, like
I'm going to first chance I
get.

MATT

I went away to school. I always
planned on coming back after
graduation.

NANCY

For what? To work in the mines
like everyone else?

MATT

You know I won't go down
there.

NANCY

You're not the first kid who
lost his dad in the mines.
Damn place will kill my dad,
it's just takin' a bit longer.
He can't walk ten feet without

hackin' and coughin' up a
lung.

GRANDPA

I'm not talkin' about the
mines killin' people, it's
something else.

NANCY

What's he talking about?

MATT

Somebody stole my Grandmother's
body.

NANCY

What?

MATT

Someone...

GRANDPA

Or something...

MATT

...or something stole grandma's
body from the morgue.

NANCY

Oh my God.

GRANDPA

God ain't here no more. God
ain't been in Draiden for a
long time.

MATT

Funeral is suppose to be
tomorrow.

                    NANCY
That's horrible.

                    MATT
Sheriff is out looking for
her now.

                    NANCY
Good luck with that, Sheriff's
related to everyone around
here, good and bad. He ain't
gonna arrest nobody.

                    MATT
Somebody crossed the line on
this.

                    NANCY

**(Finishes beer, shakes it from side to side to confirm that it's
empty and then crushes it loudly)**

You got anything to drink?

                    MATT
I don't know, like what?

                    NANCY
Like a Bloody Mary or
something.

(GRANDPA gives MATT an knowing look)

                    MATT
You still keep the beer out
back Grandpa?

                  GRANDPA
Yeah.

>   **MATT**
> Back porch in the fridge, I'll
> get it for you.

>   **NANCY**
> That's ok, I'll get it.

(NANCY exits out back, GRANDPA hurries over to MATT)

>   **GRANDPA**
> See, she's one of them.

>   **MATT**
> What are you talking about?

>   **GRANDPA**
> Just look at her, she looks
> like one of them undead
> things.

>   **MATT**
> That's make-up Grandpa, she's
> into Goth. She's just dressed
> up for the party.

>   **GRANDPA**
> It's a feeding party. You can't
> go. She asked for blood.

>   **MATT**
> A Bloody Mary, Gramps, tomato
> juice,vodka, you know, with a
> celery stick and a cocktail
> onion.

>   **GRANDPA**
> She's one of them. She's
> evil.

(GRANDPA grabs stake)

MATT

She is not.

GRANDPA

What do you know about her?
What do you really know?

MATT

What do you mean? We dated
all through high school, even
talked about getting married,
she's fine.

GRANDPA

She might have changed. You
haven'L seen her in four years,
she could have (pause) you
know, become one of them.

(The SHERIFF knocks forcefully at the front door, startling them both.)

GRANDPA (CONT)

They're here, they're here to
get us Matt.

(GRANDPA goes over to the wood pile and grabs several stakes and hands some to MATT who takes them reluctantly)

SHERIFF

(SHERIFF pounds on door forcefully)

Willis, open up, I need to
talk to you.

MATT

What do we do?

GRANDPA

(GRANDPA hides behind the door with his stakes ready to kill)

He's gonna kill us, Matt, and
we'll end up like them.

SHERIFF

(SHERIFF pounds on the door again)

Willis, I know you're in
there, open the door!

GRANDPA

You're gonna have to decide
Matt, I'm not gonna be like
them, I'm not going to turn
into a monster.

MATT

Grandpa, it's the Sheriff.

GRANDAP

I'll kill you if I have to,
if you turn into one of them,
I'll put a stake right through
you.

SHERIFF

(SHERIFF pounding on the door)

Come on Willis, open up, don't
make me kick this door in.

GRANDPA

Decide.

MATT

What do you want me to do?

GRANDPA

Open the door and step back,
I'll get him when he comes
in.

MATT

(MATT steps up and opens the door slightly and backs away hesitantly. The SHERIFF opens the door and takes a few steps inside, he does not see GRANDPA behind the door. GRANDPA slowly raises the stake to drive it through the SHERIFF's chest from behind. NANCY walks in the back door, sees GRANDPA about to kill the SHERIFF.)

NANCY

(screams!)

(the SHERIFF steps aside and GRANDPA lunges and falls to the ground)

MATT

(MATT charges the SHERIFF with a stake in his hand, screaming)

AHHHHHHHHH!

NANCY

Matt, don't!

                            MATT
                      (MATT hesitates)

                           SHERIFF

(SHERIFF draws his gun and points it at MATT, MATT stops)

              Don't make me shoot you boy.
              Now, put that stick down.

                            MATT
              Are you going to kill me,
              Sheriff?

                           SHERIFF
              I will if you don't put that
              stick down, now do it.

                            MATT

**(MATT drops the stick and stands there, defeated, the SHERIFF
relaxes a little. GRANDPA sits up on the floor, he has lost the fight
in him)**

                           SHERIFF

(SHERIFF looks at NANCY)

              What's going on here?

                           NANCY
              They think something's loose
              in the town, something from
              the mine.

                           SHERIFF
              Oh, the monsters.

GRANDPA

Feeders. You know something's out there Sherriff, something evil from the mine, it took my son, took your son too.

SHERIFF

Cave-ins took our sons, Willis, the mines have killed a lot people. Don't you think I grieve everyday for my boy, like you do yours?

GRANDPA

(sobs)

The damn mine took my son, Sheriff. It took my boy.

SHERIFF

The mines are dangerous, and we've all lost someone in that hole, but they knew what they were getting into, they knew the risks and they took their pay, same as they took their chances, but there ain't nothin' evil out there, Willis, no conspiracy, no vampires, no monsters.

GRANDPA

Something's happening to this town Sheriff.

SHERIFF

It's change Willis. Change is happening to Draiden, like everywhere else in the world.

GRANDPA

It wasn't supposed to happen here.

SHERIFF

It happens everywhere. That's life.

GRANDPA

Not my son, not my wife.

SHERIFF

We found your wife, Willis.

MATT

You found Grandma's body?

SHERIFF

Yeah, in the shed behind this house. She had a stake through her heart.

MATT

How'd she get in the shed?

SHERIFF

You got anything you want to say Willis?

GRANDPA

I couldn't let her be turned into one of them things.

SHERIFF

Someone saw your grandfather's
truck drive off from the morgue
this morning. That's when they
discovered your grandmother's
body missing.

MATT

He said he didn't want her to
turn into a Feeder.

SHERIFF

There are no monsters here.
Is that what all those stakes
are for, monster killing?

MATT

He thought this town was filled
with evil.

SHERIFF

That's a lot of stakes.

MATT

He was planning on killing
the whole town.

(SHERIFF looks at GRANDPA with a sad look)

SHERIFF

There's no monsters in this
town, Willis, good people
live here, people you've
known all your life. (to MATT)
You stick around, I'll have
some questions for you in
the morning. Come on Willis,
let's go.

(GRANDPA stands up slowly and the SHERIFF grabs GRANDPA by the arm and takes him through the front door)

MATT

(in shock, he sits on the couch)

> I can't believe all this, it's crazy, he wanted me to help him kill everyone; he thought you were one of them too. Grandpa was crazy, he thought the whole town had turned into...Feeders.

NANCY

(NANCY walks behind MATT and picks up the big hunting knife and admires it affectionately)

> You're grandpa is crazy.

MATT

(talking about the knife)

> What are you doing with that?

NANCY

> This? I thought you knew, I'm one of them Matt. I want you.

MATT

> What?

NANCY

Oh silly, (puts knife down), I'm just kidding. You're not starting to believe all this are you?

MATT

(Sudden loud howling of the wolves, very closc).

Do you hear that?

NANCY

Hear what?

MATT

The wolves. I hear the howling of the wolves outside, someone will die by dawn.

NANCY

I don't hear anything.

MATT

Grandpa was right, evil has come to Draiden and they're here for us.

(There is a sudden, loud pounding on the door. The wolves cry. NANCY hears the sound this time. NANCY and MATT look at one another.)

LIGHTS OUT

Story Notes

SLICES OF LIFE
Twisted Tales and Nasty Endings Volume III

SPOILER ALERTS

Scrap Booking for Cannibals-Thought of the title and had to write a story to go with it.

The Factory-Another older story that evolved over time, a graphic novel, the original ending was much darker, but on rewrite, I liked this better.

The Spider-There are big terrors and little terrors and sometimes it's the little things that matter.

End of the Line-I saw an older gentlemen from across the room, he was waiting on something or for someone. He wasn't that old, he didn't look that sick or crippled, he just looked sad. He was way past his prime, career over, kids gone, health fading, he just looked sad, he looked like he was just waiting for death. I saw him and wrote this story about how his demeanor made me feel.

Big Billy Boggus's Bestest Job-This started out to be one of those gross horror stories where realization collides with reality and the big "Uh-Oh" smashes us in the face, but Billy gets hit with lemons and tastes lemonade.

The Obliquity of the Ecliptic-I kind of wondered what would happen if all this stuff we produce, people, pollution, used cars, old ice boxes, plastic water bottles, everything got too much for the earth to sustain and knocked us off balance. This story was first published by Amazon.com Amazon Shorts Program.

Amazon Shorts are short stories and short articles on a huge variety of topics from horror, humor, science fiction, business, self improvement, history and everything else from well known to unknown authors for just .49 cents. You can download it to your PDA, PC, laptop, etc and you own it from now on, you can download it as many times as you want. It is a great way to try new authors and revisits some of your favorites.

Tribes-I promise not to write any more stories about cannibals.

   I promise not to write any more stories about cannibals.

   I promise not to write any more stories about cannibals.

   I promise not to write any more stories about cannibals.

   I promise not to write any more stories about cannibals.

Shower Noise-Hasn't this happened to you? You get in the shower, lather up and then hear the phone ring only to get out and run in the other room and find no one's called? Or you hear voices or footsteps you know are not in your house but you get out to investigate anyway and wind up making a mess on your carpet. This is a what-if story.

Laramie-This is sort of Twilight Zone'esque in the way people respond to fantastical situations. What would you do, go or stay?

The Finger (originally titled F@*K YOU!)-Nobody likes getting "the finger," and usually you don't even know what it is that pissed someone off, you look up and you've done something so bad as to makes someone else mad enough to "shoot you the finger." To me, it's disturbing, can be infuriating and can lead to violence. So what if there was more to it than that, what if that anger, that finger had power, would you use it? And what if there was a limit to that power or what if everyone had that same power, would you then use it or would we have peace through equal firepower?

The Slush Pile-This is simply writer's revenge. Next up, critics.

Tribes-I always wonder about the hierarchy of society, why do they pay athletes more than doctors? Or CEO's more than Sergeants? There are answers as to pay scales, education, supply and demand, ability, past successes, but what if society were turned upside down, where would all the skill sets shake out?

Fame-Forbes publishes a report of the top-earning Dead Celebrities every year and Elvis is usually at the top. Others like cartoonist Charles Schultz, musicians Jimmy Hendrix, John Lennon and Bob Marley usually make the list. These guys are still making millions long after they are gone, so what's the real price of fame?

Snippets-Snippets are real short stories, around 1000 words, give or take that needed telling, but didn't take a whole lot of words to do it. I liked these story ideas but did not feel the idea warranted a lot of back story, plot development, characterization to get to the punch line, so they are really short. Enjoy.

The Fear-A Play in One Act-This started out as a novella and then turned into a play and was featured in the Tyler Civic Theatre's third annual festival of plays. I didn't know how horror would work on the stage but after some great performances by the actors, the piece left plenty of people a little freaked out.

Graphic Arts by Charles Smith Graphics–The four graphics in this book were created by Charles Smith, a good friend and great artist. I have always enjoyed the collaborative process. I am always blown away when seeing my ideas expressed in art or on the stage with the actor or artist bringing their talents and vision to the idea.

BIO PAGE

▼

Emmitte Hall

Mr. Hall is a writer, photographer and playwright living in the piney woods of Texas. He has published over 200 articles and photographs on everything from technology, health, the internet, restaurant and movie reviews and the local music scene. His plays have had readings in Texas, California, Ohio and Florida. He holds a Bachelors and a Masters degree.

This is the third book in the Twisted Tales and Nasty Ending series.

Visit him on the web at **www.emmittehall.com**